D0320388

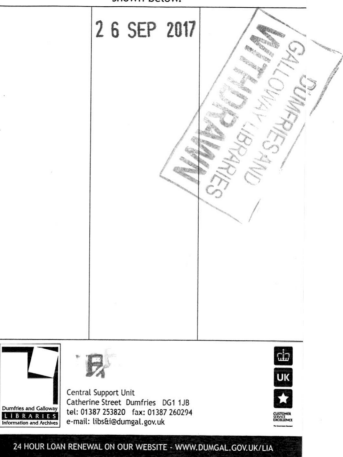

AS
DOHA
SAID

AS DOHA SAID

Bahaa Taher

Translated by Peter Daniel

ARABIA BOOKS
LONDON

First published in Great Britain in 2009 by
Arabia Books
70 Cadogan Place
London SW1X 9AH
www.arabia-books.co.uk

This edition published by arrangment with
The American University in Cairo Press
113 Sharia Kasr el Aini, Cairo, Egypt
420 Fifth Avenue, New York, NY 10018
www.aucpress.com

ISBN 978-1-906697-16-7

Printed in the UK by J F Print Ltd., Sparkford, Somerset
Cover design: Arabia Books
Page design: AUC Design Centre
Cover image: Getty Images

1

It was several years past the dawn of Egypt's 1952 revolution. The noise that once shaped the rhythm of life in our office had suddenly stopped.

Our mornings used to start with the rumble coming from inside the stock exchange. Later in the day, when it erupted into the street, we'd know that it was almost time for us to clock out too.

There was a musical structure to that noise. It started off slowly in a soft collective murmur like the chanting of a communal prayer. Soon, the tempo accelerated and the pitch escalated to a tumultuous roar, above which soared a solitary voice, shrill and strident, yet sustaining a neutral, monotonous pace that somehow ordered the clamor of words and numbers called out from below. Then, at the peak of the crescendo: silence, as abruptly as rowdy children clamming up the moment a stern teacher enters the classroom. After a brief interlude, blaring car horns and the shouts of people calling out to one another in the street punctuated loud conversations resumed with argumentative heat.

Personally, I never understood what went on in that building. However, like my colleagues, I had grown accustomed to working amid the din. Then came that summer morning in the early 1960s—the day after the nationalization decrees—when we were engulfed in silence. The atmosphere at work was eerie. We found that we had to keep lowering our voices because we had grown used to having to shout in order make ourselves heard.

I stood at the window that overlooked the vacant, narrow street behind the stock exchange building. Doha came over and stood next to me.

"What are you thinking about?" she asked.

"The silence."

She laughed, something which had not occurred often since she'd started working with us several months earlier. "I feel odd, too. I was as used to that noise as people who live by the sea are used to the sound of the waves. Then when it stopped. . . ."

She didn't complete her thought. I thought she was about to say, "The sea dried up." Instead, she said, as she contemplated the empty street below, "Maybe Sayyid has more to worry about than we do."

Only two cars were parked down there. Sayyid, the parking attendant, was sitting between them on the curb, his folded hands resting in the lap of his gallabiya. He had unbuttoned the yellow sportsjacket he always wore over his village garb no matter how hot the weather.

"Look at him," Doha said, gazing at him in wonder, "sitting on the edge of the pavement like a suspended tear."

"Are you upset about what happened?" I asked.

She jerked back as though stung. "Me? Why should I be upset?" She turned and headed back to her desk, slapping the palms of her hands as though wiping off dust. "Since they took our land, we have nothing left to lose. The same with my husband. He has nothing left either."

Her husband would crop up in every other sentence or so in her conversation. Maybe that's why I had yet to admit to myself that I loved her.

After resuming her place at her desk she said, "Still, I'm for the revolution."

I laughed dryly as I returned to my desk, which was opposite hers. She looked straight at me, her dark eyes gleaming, "I'm not joking. I'm telling the truth. In the French and Russian revolutions, in sophisticated Europe, they chopped the heads off the likes of us. Here I have a job with the revolutionary government. How could I be against it? Are you against it?"

"Whether I'm for it or against it is not important. I'm just a civil servant. Anyway, I don't know much about politics, and I don't want to."

This was not quite true. I was once almost addicted to politics. But, that was long ago.

A wry smile played on Doha's lips as she shook her head, reopened the book she'd been reading, and intoned toward the open pages, "It's not the ones who are 'for' or 'against' that ruin the world, but the ones who stand on the sidelines."

I gave little thought to her remark and turned my attention to the papers on my desk. Occasionally, I'd look up to steal a glance at her eyes. They confused me, those eyes. They could be so placid, almost vapid. Perhaps it was those drooping black eyelashes that made them seem vacant and submissive. But, when looking directly into your face as she spoke, those eyes would gleam, revealing another Doha, a more beautiful Doha—a Doha I was almost afraid to approach.

The street was quiet when I left work that day. Sayyid stood on the pavement, smoking a cigarette, lost in thought. His eyes that day seemed even more sunken in the deep sockets formed by the jutting cheekbones and brows of his angular and dark-skinned face. I offered some solicitous remark as I passed. He turned his head slowly toward me and said, "I'll be all right." However, the next day I caught sight of him leaning despondently on the display case fronting Mustafa's cigarette kiosk, and I overheard him say, "I don't know what I'm going to do, Mustafa."

Several days later, when I stopped to buy a pack of cigarettes from Mustafa, Sayyid turned to me and said that he wanted to ask me a favor. He broke off and glanced at Mustafa who nodded encouragingly and said, "Go ahead, speak. There's nothing to be afraid of." Sayyid began to mumble something about his faith in God and how he knew that God would look after him, but . . . . Then, he burst out, "I'm for the government, sir."

I suppressed a smile and said, "We're all for the government, Sayyid." To my surprise and embarrassment I realized that I, too, had raised my voice.

Placing his hand over his heart, Sayyid drew closer. "I'm serious," he said gravely. "I am with the government. I'm against feudalism and the proxies of colonialism, like the president says. But I have a wife and children to take care of and my situation, as you can see, is . . . ."

Mustafa cut him off. "Why are you giving him a speech, Sayyid? Just get to the point." Then he turned to me and said, "As you can see, sir, business in this street is dead. When Sayyid asked for a transfer, his boss turned him down."

"Who's his boss?" I asked.

Mustafa chuckled softly. "They even have a syndicate chief, sir. A parking attendant can't move to another street without his say-so. Sayyid's boss said, 'That's your lot, Sayyid. You have to take the bitter with the sweet.'"

"What 'sweet'?" Sayyid broke in. His sullen frown made his face seem darker. "People think that those brokers would reach into their pockets and shower me with fistfuls of money. Nobody would believe me if I said that they always paid me exactly one piaster for the parking fare. It didn't matter whether they made a profit or a loss, I never got more than a single piaster from any of them." Sayyid's mouth twisted into a bitter smile. "When the brokers were here, people envied me. After they left, they screwed me over. God damn them all!"

"Do you want Him to make things worse than they are, Sayyid?" Mustafa said. "Forget the brokers and get to the point, like I told you. And don't forget to mention that your draft status permits you to work and that you have a primary school certificate."

Sayyid perked up. "And, I'll be getting the preparatory school certificate this year, God willing," he said with renewed confidence.

Then he got to the point: could I help him get a job at the ministry? I replied that I couldn't promise anything, but I'd try.

I turned to Mustafa and asked, "What are you going to do? The brokers used to be your customers too."

He flicked his hand dismissively and said, with a hint of sarcasm, "I still have the ministry employees to depend on." Then he laughed.

2

The first person to spring to mind when Sayyid asked me to help him find a job in the ministry was Hatem.

Hatem was my lifelong friend. We'd been classmates in King Fu'ad I Secondary School and then in the Faculty of Law. After graduation we were hired by the same ministry. But it was not so much our attendance at the same schools that brought us together as it was the protest demonstrations that took place so often in those years before the revolution. Because Hatem was so tall, he and another demonstrator of similar height would often be designated to carry other comrades on their broad shoulders. For my part, I had something of a talent for composing chants and slogans.

"School's a sin today!" a voice would bellow from somewhere in the building and echo through the corridors. Classroom doors would fling open one after the other and students would pour out and amass in the schoolyard where speakers proclaimed the reasons why it was wrong to bury our heads in our studies that day. Generally, it was some nationalist cause that summoned us: "Out with the British if it costs our last drop of blood!" "Unity for the Nile Valley and the people of the Nile!" and so forth. But we also felt that it was our duty to set the rest of the world right. When British foreign secretary Bevin pressed Iraq into signing a mutual defense pact against the wishes of the Iraqi people, we, too, voiced our discontent: "If Egypt got burned by Bevin, the Portsmouth Treaty will be Bevin's grave!" Or, if Jews killed some Palestinians in Haifa, we'd rally to the cry, "Your martyrs are in heaven, Haifa. We'll avenge you, Palestine!"

Once fired up, we'd storm out of the schoolyard and into the main street, fists punching the air as we boomed out our chants for Egypt, for Palestine, for Tunisia, for Syria—for the entire East. When we caught sight of the students from Khalil Agha Secondary approaching from the opposite direction, we'd pause and listen to their chants to see whose were stronger and catchier. As the two groups drew closer, our rival chants grew louder and louder, vying in patriotic fervor. We were two roaring waves thundering toward each other, and when they crashed, it was with a tumultuous cheer. Complete strangers embraced, patted their comrades on the back, and joined forces in throwing stones at any British shops they came across—or French shops, depending on the calling of our student strike that day. Then, we'd commandeer the first tram we came across and order the driver to take us to Ismailiya Square or to Fu'ad I University, whichever best suited the occasion.

Once, we were demonstrating in Ismailiya Square, renamed Tahrir Square after liberation. We had converged on the British barracks compound, situated where the Nile Hilton Hotel and the Arab League now stand. "Down with Bevin!" and "Out with the British!" we proclaimed to those dismal, fading red-brick buildings with their tall, narrow windows still masked by blue blackout paint from the days of the war. We were separated from the compound by a high wall. Sharp spikes of brown and green shards of glass had been embedded into the top of the wall and on top of them was strung a long coil of barbed wire. The compound seemed abandoned; the buildings stood silent, all their windows shut.

I was the first to see one of those blue windows fly open to reveal a khaki-clad soldier. His face was flushed red and he was pointing a rifle at us. Hatem was standing next to me, at least a head taller than everyone else. I flung myself against him and we tumbled to the ground just as a bullet whistled by. It had only shaved off a corner of his eyebrow before burying itself somewhere in the ground behind us.

But people did die in Ismailiya Square that day.

Neither Hatem nor I had belonged to a political party before the revolution. Afterward—soon after we had started working for the ministry—he joined the Liberation Rally Organization, while I gave up politics altogether. Still, we remained close. Because of his unique gift for memorizing administrative laws and regulations, Hatem was promoted to deputy director of the personnel department, which advanced him two grades above me.

I called on him the day after Sayyid spoke with me. His office, on the fifth floor of the ministry building, was decorated to suit his rank. Unlike ours, it was fitted out with a plush carpet, chairs upholstered in leather, and a gilt-framed color photograph of the president who peered out from the wall behind his head. From the window of his office you could see the old Radio and Broadcasting Building. It was a well-proportioned structure with large brownstone blocks interspersed with broad but closely spaced windows. It looked strangely out of place amid the modern cement high-rises crowded around it, a vestige from an alien civilization.

After listening to my account of Sayyid's situation, Hatem asked, "Who's he to you?"

"All I know is that he's in a real bind. So if you can help him, why don't you?"

He laughed. "Our duty is to solve the problems of the people. I'll see what I can do. Maybe I can get him hired as a part-time office boy."

That task completed, I asked whether Hatem had heard any news about my scholarship application. Turning and heading back to his desk, he said, "You're something else. You could have had that grant years ago. In fact, you could have already been to Rome and back years ago. All your paperwork's ready, but whenever the ball starts rolling you doze off. Why don't you do something? Why don't you make some contacts?"

I smiled. "Well, I just contacted you, didn't I? You're a prominent member of the National Union Party, aren't you?"

He smiled and retorted, "So why don't you become a member, too?"

"Sure, and find several piasters' worth of membership dues docked from my salary at the beginning of every month."

"Just like my office boy. But really, you're an educated man and you know foreign languages. So why don't you take some action?"

I asked what action I should take exactly, but his attention had strayed back to his desk. As I stood up to leave I said, "By the way, I read in the papers that they're going to change the name of the National Union to the Socialist Union."

This triggered another laugh. Rising to see me off he said, "National Union, Socialist Union, Blue Devils' Union—it makes no difference. We're with them to the bitter end." He paused suddenly, struck by an idea. "Listen, I'll tell you what you can do. First, you leave that graveyard you're working in and get transferred here to ministry headquarters. Mix with people and then nominate yourself in the next staff elections. I'm telling you to change. Please."

"But the grant is designated for staff from my department. I can't leave it now. You know how much I need that grant."

After a moment's thought, Hatem's face broke into a crafty smile. "Then get Madam Doha to use her influence."

I dropped the hand I'd been shaking and scowled at him. He raised his arms in mock self-defense and said in a low confiding voice, "That woman's very well connected. She came from outside the party ranks. She was appointed at a high salary grade, and by a decree signed by the deputy minister himself. You wouldn't know who pulls the strings for her, would you?"

"What kind of person do you take me for?" I snapped. "I don't use other people like that, especially women."

"Hey, I was only joking. Why are you always so on edge?" He reached out to shake my hand again and said, "Anyway, I'll see what I can do for Sayyid. As for you, it looks like you have a long wait ahead of you."

Back in my office, Doha took one look at me and asked what was wrong. I told her about the problem with the study grant. She laughed. "Are you that desperate to get to Europe? What do you really hope to gain there—academic knowledge or knowledge of European women?"

"Since you're so concerned for my welfare, what I'm really interested in is the travel expenses. I have a sister who's probably going to get married soon and I need the money. Are you happy now?" I thumped the files I was carrying onto my desk and blew the air out of my cheeks.

Doha's smile vanished and her face flushed. "I'm sorry. I was just trying to get you to lighten up."

Meeting my stubborn silence, she turned toward the window and said in an even voice, "Don't whine about your problems. I don't like people who whine about their problems. I need money too. If only you knew how much!"

I gaped at her in disbelief, but her gaze remained fixed on the window, seemingly remote and lost in thought. Eventually, she turned her attention back to the novel she'd been reading. I knew it was *L'Espoir* by André Malraux. She bowed her head over it and her beautiful face disappeared beneath her mantle of thick black hair.

I decided to offer a gesture of reconciliation. Trying to make my voice sound light I said, "By the way, Malraux was a socialist when he wrote that novel. You'll find he has a lot to say about the ills of money."

"I know," she replied curtly without lifting her head from the book.

Yet, Doha and I grew closer that day. Before then, we had never talked about anything but work and other mundane trivialities.

We had very few office tasks to keep us occupied, which is why we had so much time for leisure reading. This "graveyard" of ours, as Hatem called it, had a history. In the early days of the revolution, the first newly appointed head of our ministry was fired by the zeal to restructure and streamline. He called a meeting of all the staff members with foreign language expertise, handed out some books on administrative organization, and outlined his 'philosophy,' which essentially was that every job and every department had to have specifically designated functions and duties. Our instructions were to draw up diagrams and flowcharts delineating job descriptions, hierarchies, conditions for promotion and the like. He then rented this apartment in a building near ministry headquarters, converted it into our office, and bestowed on us the title, "The Supervisory Board for Administrative Organization." He also authorized in-service training grants that would enable members of our department to attend business administration courses in Europe.

By the time we finished our assignment he had left the ministry. Although his replacement had not the slightest interest in our work, he kept us in our office, and I kept the organizational diagrams we had drawn up stuffed in a drawer in my desk. Eventually, most of my colleagues managed to finagle their way back to their old departments, leaving me and two or three others in the small office. Once in a while, a new colleague would arrive, exiled from his department for having fallen afoul of his boss, only to return to his original post once his boss's wrath had subsided. Sometimes the minister's office or other departments in the ministry would have us translate reports or other documents because word had spread of our foreign language expertise. Otherwise, very little work came our way.

Still, I stayed put in the hope of receiving approval for the grant to which I had been nominated. When the ministry hired Doha, they posted her in my department, since her sole qualification was her knowledge of foreign languages. I fell in love with her immediately.

That first minor flare-up must have broken a barrier, because afterward we began to tell each other about our personal lives. It was also then that we began to leave the office together and walk to Tahrir Square, where I would catch the bus to Abbasiya while she continued on foot over Qasr al-Nil Bridge to her home in Zamalek. That summer, when we began this routine, was the summer when women's hemlines first rose above the knees. Men would ogle women's long legs, thigh muscles flexing as they strolled down the sidewalks, while the women sustained a leisurely pace, pausing to gaze into shop window displays and feigning indifference to the stares and occasional crude remarks issuing from male pedestrians and passing cars. As we walked down Qasr al-Nil Street, I tried to keep my eyes dead center, but Doha would nudge me, jerk her chin at an attractive woman in the latest fashion, shoot her eyes to my face, and watch it grow flustered. She found this quite entertaining.

"What if I came to work tomorrow in a skirt like that?" she asked me one day. She giggled at my dumbfounded stare and said, "Don't you like bold women?"

"Yes, but . . . ," I stammered.

"But what?"

"It's provocative."

"Why? Haven't you seen pictures of the pharaohs and their wives? The ancient Egyptians were very pious, by the way."

"But this is Cairo, today, not Thebes thousands of years ago."

"Right," she said with a crisp nod. "Thanks for reminding me. Let's go get a coffee."

We'd reached Suleiman Pasha Square. We went into a small café next to a newspaper kiosk. The café owner—a European—hastened over to Doha, and asked in French, "As usual, madame?" "Yes, two," she answered, also in French.

After serving the coffee, he stood behind the wooden counter to await her approval. She took a sip and nodded. "Perfect." The man smiled and moved to the other end of the counter to resume his seat behind the cash register. We drank our coffee in silence, standing at the counter, our backs to the constant bustle in the square. We were the only customers in the café. After a while, Doha asked, "Why haven't you married yet? Is it because of your sister?"

"It's two sisters, not one."

"How old are you?"

"Thirty-six."

"Like my husband, almost."

She smiled and, raising an index finger to emphasize the point, added, "And I'm much younger than both of you."

She did, in fact, look younger than thirty.

When we finished our coffee, I paid the bill. However, before we left, Doha reached into her purse, pulled out a bank note worth much more than the entire bill, and handed it to the café owner. He gave a dignified smile and nodded his gratitude. Outside in the street again, she said, "He's one of the brave ones." She ignored my raised eyebrows.

As we neared Tahrir Square, where we would go our separate ways, she said, "Anyway, you have to get married."

"Yes," I answered.

She laughed and said, "You don't always have to agree with me. You can say, for example, marriage is a curse, that you'll never get married as long as you live—you know, the type of things that confirmed bachelors say." She laughed again, and added, "And married men too!"

"All right. I want to see my sisters married. That's all that matters to me right now."

"And after they marry?"

"I haven't thought that far ahead."

We stopped by the floral clock in Tahrir Square. The adjacent fountain imbued the air with a fine mist. Doha did not seem in a hurry, and I was ready to stay there forever.

Doha asked, "Haven't you given any thought to your future? Don't you have a plan for getting what you want out of life?"

"To tell the truth, Doha, I don't even know what I want out of life. I'll tell you something else. It's been a long time since I ever really wanted anything badly. I really can't say when that began. In university, I was a real go-getter, a straight-A student and my professors expected me to go on to graduate school. And that's what I wanted, too. In fact, I'd already written up a proposal for an ambitious master's thesis on law and the concept of freedom.

"But suddenly I lost interest in all that. University life and burying myself in books no longer held any appeal. Later, after I was hired by the ministry and appointed to our department, I never applied for a promotion or a transfer. Hatem was different; he was determined to work his way up the ladder. So he applied to a posting in the oases under another ministry in order to move up a pay grade. By the time he returned, he'd saved up enough money to marry, which he did—to the woman he'd loved since university. Then, after finishing his postgraduate studies, he was promoted again. Hatem says I lack ambition, and I suppose he's right. I don't even know why people have ambitions."

"Then why were you so upset about the grant?"

"Didn't I tell you? So I can afford to get my sisters married. That's why I need the money. My salary is enough to cover everything else. My rent's cheap and books are cheap. That's all I need."

Suddenly she spat out, "You're lying!"

Her outburst hadn't been that loud, but it had turned the heads of a few people waiting at the nearby bus stop, making me feel uncomfortable. I watched her walk off slowly toward the bridge, then caught up and walked beside her. At the far corner of the small garden, she veered right toward the Hilton, instead of continuing over the bridge on her usual way home. Her face was pinched with anger and she kept muttering, "Liar, liar." She made it sound as though I had hurled the insult at her.

"What makes you think I'm a liar?" I asked.

After a brief pause, she shook her head as though to clear it and said, "You remind me of the fable of the fox who couldn't reach the grapes, so he said they were sour. I think you're like Faust. You thirst for knowledge in order to own the world."

I thought about this for a moment and then said, "Well, perhaps I do want something . . . ."

"Out with it."

"I confess. But, it's not money, professional advancement, or fame. Sometimes I'm filled with anger at myself and at my life. Sometimes I'm overwhelmed by a sense of longing, but I can't put my finger on what I long for."

"Humility's great, if it's genuine. But, I've never known anybody who truly wanted something from the depth of their heart and didn't get it."

Her tone had changed again. If, earlier, her sudden outburst threw me, now it was the low, flat voice that betrayed no emotion. "I'll tell you something about the closest person to me — my husband. When we married, he had everything — youth, wealth, fame. Before the revolution he was a prominent member of the Wafd Party and he had a powerful position in the government — Director of the Office of the Minister, or something like that. All the strings in the ministry passed through his hands. Then the revolution came, and they took away his land, and mine, too. But he didn't let that get to him. We had enough money left to keep ourselves in comfort, he said. But when they kicked him out of the ministry and pensioned him off, like they did to many others at the time, he couldn't believe what had happened. I think it still hasn't sunk in. Anyway, that was when he started to gamble. And he hasn't stopped. Maybe he feels that winning a fortune will compensate for what he lost when they kicked him out. But he never wins. I mean, have you ever heard of anyone who's really made a killing at gambling? Once I told him that he was resorting to Lady Luck to bring back the past. He didn't understand. We'd lost our land and everything else, but he couldn't understand."

"Is that why you work? Is that why you said you needed money?"

Doha stopped in her tracks and her eyes widened in alarm, as though stunned by the conclusion I had drawn and by the realization that she had spoken too freely. "I can trust you, can't I? What I said is just between you and me, right?"

She seemed frantic. She kept shaking her head even as I tried to reassure her, "Yes. Yes. You can trust me. Please trust me."

But she turned away and stared blankly at the Hilton. Suddenly, in a voice filled with pent up fury, she said, "Why did they have to build that monstrosity here, right next to the Egyptian Museum? It reminds me of a cake with blue icing. It desecrates the place."

Her observation startled me. I, too, looked toward the façade of the hotel, taking in its sprinklings of hieroglyphic birds, snakes, and wavy lines. Noting the direction of my gaze she said, "Those engravings are a desecration of the ancient script. Writing used to be . . . sacred. Not decorative frills for a . . . for a . . . ."

She turned to me abruptly and said curtly, "I'm sorry. I just can't trust men."

Then she left, her heels clicking rapidly away from me.

3

oha is beautiful. She's tall and slender. The curves of her breasts and hips protrude exactly as they should without needless exaggeration. The features of her face are harmoniously proportioned, and its deep limpid honey-colored complexion is framed by a thick mantle of silky black hair that cascades luxuriantly down either side of her long, graceful neck before plunging behind her shoulders and vanishing a long way down her back. But it was her eyes that had me mystified. Hovering above them were two long, thick eyebrows that extended across the full length of her brow, and these — to my knowledge, she had never cared to pluck or shape them — together with her long eyelashes, gave the impression that her enticingly black eyes were permanently lined with mascara. Yet she rarely used cosmetics.

Of course, I've seen women more beautiful than Doha. But when she spoke I couldn't think of any who held a candle to her. I'd stare at her, trying to hide my awe and to dissemble my love, as her melodic voice coursed through me like a subtle narcotic. I'd ask myself, has she sensed that I love her? Does it show? It probably did, but she never mentioned it.

She never showed up to work without at least one book in hand: a French novel, a volume of Chinese poetry in translation, an anthology of ancient Greek plays, a book about sculpture or about plants, a historical study. She read voraciously and rapidly. Every now and then she'd look up and recite a stanza of poetry or some lines from a play. Whenever I remarked that the book she'd been reading from had been translated into Arabic, her eyes would widen and she'd say, "Really? It's been translated into Arabic?" This response invariably annoyed me. She'd watch the irritation play out on my face and laugh.

There were days, however, when she simply set the books she brought with her on her desk and left them untouched. Her eyes would have a listless glaze that nevertheless hinted at some suppressed trouble. The red capillaries would crowd out the whites of her eyes, as though she had just been crying. She'd remain mute. Eventually, she'd draw one of her books toward her and open it to a place she'd marked, only to stare at the page blankly. I'd observe her furtively and check my urge to comment.

Once, I thought I had discovered the cause of those morose states. Doha had not shown up to work for two days and, after making some inquiries, we learned that she was in the hospital. After work, a couple of colleagues and I piled into Hatem's car and went to visit her. None of her family members were there. A nurse told us, "You can go in to see her. The danger's over. But don't stay long."

She lay in bed, her eyes closed, her face a sickly gray. A large bottle of intravenous fluids hung from a stand next to her bedstead. A thin tube conducted the fluid to a needle inserted into the back of her hand. Her eyes opened and brought us into focus. She smiled wanly and raised her free hand in greeting. While Hatem and my colleagues gathered around her to offer their sympathy and encouragement, I took hold of the clipboard suspended on the white metallic frame at the foot of her bed. Written in English were the words, "Alcohol poisoning." I flipped the page over so that no one else would see it.

As we left, Hatem whispered, "I noticed you reading the status sheet. What's wrong with her?"

"I think it's a gynecological problem—a hemorrhage or something like that."

"Maybe she had a miscarriage?"

"Could be."

Hatem smiled and patted me on the back. "Anyway, don't worry. Your colleague will be back at work soon, fit as a fiddle, and the Supervisory Board of Administrative Organization will bloom again."

When Doha returned from sick leave, I told her that if anyone asked her about her illness she should give a vague enough answer to let them understand that she didn't want to discuss the matter. I didn't elaborate and she kept her reply to a minimum: "Thank you."

But her sullen spells grew more frequent and she seemed constantly tense and irritable. It was around that time, as I recall, that she first met Sayyid.

I had already introduced Sayyid to Hatem. Sayyid had brought his various certificates and documents with him for the occasion. Several days after that meeting, Hatem told me, "Your friend's an Upper Egyptian like me. And he's full of revolutionary zeal." He emitted a loud bark of laughter, as he did whenever he spoke to me about politics. Still, in spite of Hatem's backing, it took a long while for the appointment to come through.

Sayyid was beaming when he came to visit me in my office for the first time, wearing the gray uniform of the ministry's office boys. He had come to thank me. "If you ask me to chop my arm off for you, sir, I'll do it."

At that moment, Doha entered the room and said, "Congratulations, Sayyid."

Sayyid's eyebrows shot up, apparently surprised that she knew his name. She pointed to the window and explained, "I could see you from there and would hear people calling for you."

He laughed and said, "Oh, in the days of the private sector."

"Weren't you happy in the days of the private sector?"

"Since when does degradation make people happy, ma'am? In those days, they used to call me 'Sayyid boy,' as in, 'Come here, Sayyid boy'; 'Take this, Sayyid boy.' Here I'm known as Sayyid al-Qinawi or just plain Sayyid. This gentleman here calls me Sayyid and so does Mr. Hatem."

Doha shook her head and said, "You're eloquent, too."

"No, I'm just Sayyid al-Qinawi, ma'am," he quipped.

But Doha didn't smile. She massaged her temples with her fingers and said, without looking at him, "But some of them were decent people, weren't they?"

"Decent to each other, ma'am, but not to the poor. You don't know them."

"Shut up, Sayyid," I said.

"I just want to help the lady understand. She doesn't know those people."

Doha's eyes darkened. "But even so, their money helped people live. Your income came from their charity, didn't it?"

I tried to intervene, but to no avail. Sayyid was in full swing. His jaw thrust forward, his heavy highbrows scowled, and his eyes narrowed to slits. "So, you say that too. You have no idea what their charity was like, ma'am, but I do. They'd buy bottles of whisky for I don't know how many pounds, put them in their fancy cars, and then haggle with the radish or lemon vendors over piasters. I tell you . . . ."

I took hold of Sayyid's elbow and almost forcibly led him out of the office into the vestibule. He was glowering, his eyes burning. Keeping my voice as even as I could, I tried to calm him. "Sayyid, there was no need for you to speak that way to her. She's one of *those* people."

He swung his forefinger toward his forehead and said heatedly, "What do you take me for? I could tell what she was the moment I saw her. I could tell, so I tried to educate her."

Now I flared. "Who asked you to educate her? Let her be."

"As you say, sir." But he was still angry when he left.

That was the beginning of the aversion between Doha and Sayyid.

As I stepped back into the office, Doha said, "I'm sorry. There was no cause for me to lose my temper." She issued a short hollow laugh. "But really, that was a bit too much. Sayyid al-Hinawi or al-Hifnawi or whatever his name is, prattling on about the 'private sector' and '*those* people,' and giving me a lecture!" She shook her head as though to say, "Some people!"

She hadn't met the real Sayyid yet. Nor had I for that matter. Yet over the next few months practically the entire ministry came to know who Sayyid al-Qinawi was. Hatem took him along to a meeting of the Socialist Union's political recruitment team in the ministry and soon afterward Sayyid nominated himself to the ministry's labor syndicate board. He was elected. In fact, he beat many worker candidates who had years of seniority over him and years of practice at fielding themselves in these elections. His simplicity, his ardor, and his total lack of affectation or pretense won the affection and trust of his colleagues and acquaintances in the ministry. As soon as Sayyid obtained his preparatory school certificate, Hatem helped him get appointed as labor superintendent. Now he had an office and, instead of the office boys' uniform, he wore a modest suit. I'd watched others go through this transition; in no time at all they'd puff up with self-importance and affect the airs of a government functionary. I was certain Sayyid would go the same way.

Not long after he received his new appointment, I ran into him in Hatem's office. Hatem was speaking with Sayyid emphatically, running his hands through his hair in exasperation. The moment he noticed me he held out his hands in a plea for aid. "It's a good thing you came. Tell your friend to get some sense into his head."

Sayyid, who was standing in front of Hatem's desk, turned to me and smiled. "But the Bey agrees with me, sir," he said to Hatem. Then to me, "Don't you agree, sir, that workers are still alive on Fridays like the rest of God's creatures?"

Hatem laughed and said, "Sayyid, this gentleman, here, buries his head in novels and poetry. You can't expect him to know anything about the Friday problem."

21

I took a seat and said, "Poetry, my good man, has not precluded my ability to realize that the ministry deducts Fridays from the salaries of the workers it hires on a daily wage basis."

"Obviously, like Sayyid, you have no conception of the whole picture. It's not just our ministry that has this problem. It's a problem in every ministry in the government and we can't solve it alone."

Sayyid said, "But, sir, you know there are articles in the ministry's budgetary regulations that could help."

Hatem shot out angrily, "Who put that idea into your head, Sayyid? What do you know about the ministry's budget?" He turned to address me. "I swear, they're already thinking about firing him because of what he gets up to. He doesn't have tenure yet, so all it would take to boot him out is a memo signed by the personnel director."

I turned to Sayyid and asked, "Can't you leave this problem to someone else? At least until you're tenured?"

"And what am I supposed to say to the people who elected me to the board, sir? Do I tell them, 'Wait till I get tenured and then I'll act like a man'? There's a saying where I come from . . . ."

Hatem raised his hands to cut him off and signal that his patience was at an end. In a jeering voice he said, "To hell with you and those like you, Sayyid al-Qinawi, and to hell with those who elected you. I mean, do you think they elected you to parliament, man? We're talking about a committee—a committee nobody's ever heard of and wouldn't hear of even if you all dropped dead tomorrow."

Sayyid laughed and retorted, "I realize I'm on a committee, not in parliament. But what else can I do? I'll tell you what. Why don't you get me into parliament? Then I'll solve all the country's problems."

The meeting ended in a stalemate.

After we left Hatem's office, Sayyid produced a folded piece of paper from his pocket and handed it to me. "Sir, this is a memorandum that the syndicate board wants to send out about the problem with payment on Fridays. We put down our ideas as best we could, but could you look it over and put in the correct government language?"

I unfolded the memo and read through it as we threaded our way through the corridors of the ministry on our way to the exit. When I finished I said, "But this is perfectly clear and well-written, Sayyid. You must be the one who wrote it."

"Yes, I was. But did you really like it? Did my education really do me any good?"

I nodded emphatically. "It certainly did. In fact, a little too good."

His smile vanished. "Are you poking fun at me, sir?"

"Not at all, I swear."

He frowned as though uncertain whether to take me at my word. "I did the best I could. After my wife and children went to bed, I'd go outside and study under the street lamp."

"And by doing that you got what you set out to achieve. What I meant was that you're taking this matter too seriously. Other people think of themselves and their families first. But you, you've only been with the ministry for a few months and already you're making trouble for yourself."

We were nearing that corridor where we had to lower our voices because at the end of it lay the red carpet that led to the minister's office. I was heading toward the stairwell just before that corridor, so I held out my hand to say good-bye, but Sayyid said, "I'll come with you."

Sayyid remained sullen as we as we walked down the stairs. But when we reached the vast entrance hall on the ground floor, which was filled with ministry staff members coming and going, he halted abruptly and asked, "Sir, do you really advise me to quit the syndicate board?"

I swung toward him and shouted, "Did I say anything of the sort, Sayyid? What do I care if you stay on the board or leave it? It's none of my business."

23

I left him and marched rapidly toward the door, but he ran after me and caught hold of my arm. "Please don't be angry with me. I'm just trying to understand."

"So this is where you ask me to help you understand? In the entrance hall in front of the entire ministry staff, so they can say that I'm turning you against the syndicate board? Do you think I don't have enough problems already, Sayyid?"

"I'm sorry, sir. I just wasn't thinking."

We left the ministry together, but without speaking. The way to my office took us by the old Radio and Broadcasting Building. In front of the squat brownstone edifice were rows of tightly packed parked cars. The parking attendant was darting back and forth, shouting instructions to car owners as he shoved other cars out of their way, pushing with his backside against the hood while keeping his feet planted on the ground, exactly as Sayyid used to do in the street behind the stock exchange. As we drew closer, Sayyid moved ahead to greet him.

"How's work these days, Mahmoud?" he asked jovially.

"Mahmoud lowered his eyes in embarrassment. "All right . . . fine, thanks be to God."

As we continued on our way, Sayyid asked, "So what's your advice, sir? You're a good man, and you're educated, and I'm still new at work, so what should I do?"

After a moment's silence I said, "Frankly, Sayyid, I don't know what advice I can give you, but at least think of your children first."

Gesturing toward the cars, he said, "Yeah, so they don't grow up chasing after cars in the street like their father."

"Now that you're a government employee, you can bring your children up to be better than that."

"And what if something were to happen to me tomorrow?"

We were nearing the apartment block where my office was. Sayyid came to a stop and stared down at the pavement at his feet. I stood beside him, unable to continue on my way because

I felt he had something more to tell me. He did. "Do you remember what the lady who works with you in your office said? She said that I used to live off of *their* charity. But I'm going to tell you a story. In our village in Upper Egypt, my father really did live off their charity. He was a farmhand who worked the land of the rich. We were dirt poor: the only times we ever tasted bread made of wheat was at harvest time; the rest of the year we ate cornmeal bread. When wheat bread entered our home, it was like a feast. But that's not why my father left the village. One evening we were coming home from the field—I'd been helping him the whole day. We were riding a donkey. I was seven or eight years old at the time. Then, he saw one of the village masters walking toward us. My father jumped off the donkey and took hold of my arm and tried to coax me down. But I was too young to understand. I didn't know that farmhands were supposed to dismount in the presence of a landlord who was on foot, or even on horseback. Baffled by what my father was doing, I stayed seated on the donkey. As the man drew up to where we were, my father raised his hand to his forehead in salute and offered a respectful greeting. But the man swung out his arm and slapped me on the face. 'Listen to what your father tells you, boy! Get down!' So I got down . . . or maybe the slap threw me down. Anyway, as the man walked off, he said to my father, without looking back, 'Teach your son some manners, Qinawi. Rudeness is the devil's work.' My father didn't reply. I cried the whole way home and my father remained totally silent. But the moment he stepped into the house he said to my mother, 'Get ready to leave, woman. We aren't going spend another night in this village.'

"The next morning he sold everything off and we took a train to Cairo. He bought a cart and started work as a roaming fruit vendor. He put me in school, but I didn't last there long. He died when I was twenty. I had younger brothers and sisters, so I had to find a job. I worked day and night. In the daytime I

25

hawked combs and chewing gum in the tramway cars and in the evenings I helped a parking attendant. But the few piasters I earned weren't enough, so my mother had to take my brothers and sisters back to the village and move in with her relatives there. I sent them all the money I could, and I still do. As I grew older I began to realize that life in Cairo was no different from the life my father thought he'd left behind in the village. Here, too, there were masters, not on horseback, but in cars. And others, like me, scrambled after them for piasters. That's the kind of charity I lived off, sir, and I don't want my children to experience it."

Sayyid was breathing heavily when he had finished telling me this. His eyes glistened damply and he fixed them on me. But my patience had worn thin. "Yes, I know that ailment, Sayyid."

"What ailment?" he asked in alarm.

I started walking again, picking up my pace and forcing Sayyid to hasten to keep up. "Listen, Sayyid. Thousands of people get slapped around every day, but only a handful of them feel insulted or angry. Very few of them succumb to that illness that infected your father and that's now infected you. It's called the itch for justice."

"I don't understand. Please explain, for God's sake. I have to learn. I'd give anything to anyone who'll teach me."

"You'll learn by yourself, Sayyid. You don't need anybody to teach you."

We reached the corner of the side street between the stock exchange and the block where I worked. Sayyid pointed to the vacant stock exchange building and its darkened windows and said, "But I do understand one thing, at least. Everything's changed. It's our country now. The revolution's made it our country and we have to help it. Isn't that right, sir?"

He looked at me for confirmation, but I said indifferently, "Maybe." Then I waved the paper he had given to me and said, "I'll rewrite this memo in government style. You can stop by tomorrow and pick it up." I left him standing at the corner and headed quickly toward my office.

But Sayyid didn't show up at my office the following day, or the day after. Fearful that they may have indeed fired him, I called up Hatem to inquire.

"Haven't you heard? The army's called him up. He's probably already on his way to Yemen," he informed me.

"Yemen? But what about his children?"

"That doesn't prevent one from doing one's duty, my good man. We're at war now. Anyway, who knows? Maybe it's better for his children this way; the pay's better over there."

"Okay, sure. But he left this memo with me about the Friday problem. What should I do with it?"

He chuckled and said, "How about crumpling it up and tossing it in the Nile?"

"Perhaps I should give it to his colleagues on the board?"

"Whatever. Just leave me out of it. Anyway, his colleagues are more sensible."

I replaced the receiver and stared at it silently for a moment. Without tearing herself away from the book she was reading, Doha asked, "Who went to Yemen?"

"Sayyid al-Qinawi."

"Poor guy," she said dismissively.

"He has children, and, from what I understood from him, there's no one else to support them. His brothers are all back in their village in Upper Egypt where they have jobs."

Now she glanced up. "I see. So your heart can bleed too."

The sudden broadside indicated that I should drop the subject.

But she didn't. "Even so, maybe that's as it should be. From what I understood from him and from others, he's a true believer in the revolution. Why shouldn't he defend it, even if it takes him to Yemen?"

If it was not that day, it was very soon afterward that Doha and I were walking down Qasr al-Nil after work when she suddenly stopped, blanched, and muttered in a barely audible voice, "That one too?"

She was staring at a barren shop window on which was posted a sign that read, "Commercial Premises for Sale—Stock and Fixtures Included." She shook her head in disbelief and said softly, "Even Sistovariç is leaving?"

I didn't utter a word, but Doha snapped her head toward me as though I had just flung out an insinuating remark. "It's not because he's a furrier. I couldn't care less about furs. I never wear them. But look at this street. Only yesterday a shimmering silver fur radiated from this shop window on the corner, and now . . . I mean . . . . Do you understand what I'm trying to say? Streets have lives, too. Their parts are like body parts; when one disappears it's as though it's been amputated."

Doha pointed in the direction of Shawarbi Street. "Do you see that building? There was an outdoor café there once, screened off from the street by a façade of trees. You'd pass through a gate, descend a few stairs, and suddenly you'd find that you'd left the city of brick and stone behind you and entered a paradise of trees and flowers. There were pathways of sparkling clean sand and tables nestled inside trellised bowers beneath the trees. I used to come here with my friends when I was a girl. I loved the trees. In fact, I think there was a magnolia that would burst into a red blaze in the spring. Was there really a magnolia or am I just imagining it? Nonetheless, since they tore down that café and put that hideous building in its place, I can't look directly at that part of the street—just like when I avert my eyes when I see someone with an amputated arm. Do you follow me? It's not because it was a fur store. How can they let that happen? Do you understand what I'm trying to say?"

"I'm trying," I said. I was embarrassed to ask her what a magnolia was.

Doha resumed walking, downcast. I walked silently beside her. Now that mini-skirted women had proliferated, they attracted fewer oglers and crude remarks, and I could look at them unabashed. Anyway, when I was with Doha I barely noticed them. I found myself thinking about the silver fur coat that had disappeared from Sistovariç's and caught myself regretting its disappearance, even as a radio from a nearby cigarette kiosk blasted out at top volume that Abd al-Halim Hafez song that goes, "You're the hero. You're the Abu Zeid of your age. Mount your steed, called 'Duty to the Nation.'" The imposingly heavyset figure of Talaat Harb glared down at me from the center of the square that bore his name—they had recently taken down the statue of Suleiman Pasha, the French-born army commander who served in the Egyptian army under Muhammad Ali, and replaced it with the statue of the nationalist industrialist who founded the Bank of Egypt—while from a ful bean and taamiya sandwich stall at an intersection in the square another radio blared out Abd al-Wahab's doleful voice singing, "When you scorn me, I call it love." The sidewalk in front of the sandwich stall was packed with customers jostling one another as they shouted out their orders. Had I not known better, I might have thought it was a political rally. I don't understand what's happening to this country, I thought. I don't understand Doha. All I know is that I love her. I don't understand myself. I should probably stop thinking altogether.

We entered the small espresso café that was always empty at this time in the afternoon. The European owner was seated on his stool in front of the cash register, looking out absentmindedly at the square and at the newly installed statue of Talaat Harb.

After we had finished our coffee, Doha said, "By the way, I never asked you how you picked up your foreign languages. You said that you had a public education, so how did you come to learn English and French so well?"

"When I first began school, my father enrolled me in a private English-language elementary school in Abbasiya. But by the time I'd finished elementary school my sisters had also begun school—in the Lycée Française. Our education was costing our father a fortune—he was an ordinary civil servant with a secondary school certificate and his means were limited—so he transferred me to a public secondary school because the fees were much lower. That's where I began to take French and I continued studying French in university."

She said, without looking at me, "But that wouldn't be enough. I think the real reason is that you read a lot."

"Maybe. That is, I used to read a lot. Now I hardly ever touch books—I mean the kind that expand your mind. Those I don't read at all."

"Why's that?"

I didn't answer immediately. I looked out at the square. For some reason Sayyid al-Qinawi came to mind and I said, "Sometimes injustice confuses me too."

My response startled her. "What made you say that? What do you mean by injustice? There are many types of injustice."

"All types of injustice. I learned the meaning of injustice when I was very young. My father was a very cruel man and my mother was a very meek woman. She'd get up at dawn, fill the bath for my father, make him breakfast, iron the clothes that he would wear to work, and then she'd do the same for my sisters and me. My father was never satisfied. From the moment he awoke he'd light into her: his ablution water was too hot or too cold; the eggs hadn't been boiled long enough; anything at all. And once he started, he wouldn't stop. He kept battering her with a stream of insults and curses until he left the house. My mother never answered back; she thought that this was his right. But I'll never forget one day when I was still in elementary school and, for some reason—perhaps I was sick—I stayed home. Nobody was there but my mother and me. My mother used to raise chickens on the roof, and that day I went up to the roof. She didn't notice me. She was sitting on a short stool,

30

tossing feed to the cluster of chickens around her, and muttering in a low voice. She was recounting to the chickens all the insults and curses my father had hurled at her that morning. And every once in a while she'd tell her little audience, "But I didn't do anything wrong! I swear to God, I didn't do anything wrong!" As I recall, I snuck away before she could see me. I ran downstairs and burst into tears. My mother died young. The domestic drudgery and the daily oppression had destroyed her. She also died quietly — without a single word of complaint. I couldn't even hate my father or blame him for what he'd done. He, too, collapsed after her death: one illness followed another until he died. I had just graduated from college at the time. He'd never tried to befriend me; in fact, he rarely spoke to me or to my sisters unless it was to give us orders or to check up on our progress at school. He was a lonely man. He was an only child and had severed relations with his cousins who lived on the west bank of the Nile, in a village just north of Cairo near the Khayriya Barrages. It was hard for him to open up to anyone, even his son. He didn't even have chickens to complain to."

Doha said, "I didn't mean to open the door to all those awful memories. Try to put them behind you." Then she smiled and a glint of mischief lit her beautiful black eyes. "But tell me, what caused your transformation into Faust?"

"So, you've latched on to that idea again?" I said, smiling in return. "What makes you keep insisting that I'm Faust? You read far more than I do. As I told you, I lost interest in reading a long time ago. Why shouldn't you be Faust?"

She fixed her sparkling eyes on me and exclaimed, "What a fantastic idea! Yes! A female Faust. Why not? Why should men be the only ones to have the right to weary of the dismal monotony of the world and rebel? Who said women can't yearn as much as, and maybe even more, than men to break free of this impossible yoke and soar after mysterious delights to the accompaniment of forbidden music? After all, wasn't it Eve who was tempted to pick the apple?"

"Are you ready to sign a contract in blood?" I asked.

At that moment my hand spontaneously reached over to touch hers, which was resting on the wooden countertop. It was a very gentle, friendly touch. But Doha jerked back her hand, almost in alarm. She would have knocked over her coffee cup had she not steadied it with her other hand.

"I'm sorry," I stammered.

"Don't be," she said. But the gleam had faded from her eyes. "I like the idea, that's all." She forced a smile. "Anyway, I can't be Faust, if only because he was so old."

"No . . . I mean, yes. He was no longer young enough to pluck the fruit, nor was he old enough to forget it."

She did not respond. She arched her eyebrows at her empty coffee cup as though it perplexed her. I turned to stare aimlessly out the window at the back of Talaat Harb.

4

I gave considerable thought, over the following days, to applying for a transfer out of the "graveyard." Perhaps by physically removing myself from Doha's presence I could eventually overcome this futile infatuation. I could not go on spending hour after hour alone with her in that office, unable to declare my feelings, without an ounce of hope even if I did, and without a soul in whom I could confide this illicit yet inescapable love. I had to put this dilemma to an end. But deep inside, I knew that I wouldn't act. I would never ask for a transfer, because every night I prayed for morning to hurry up so I could relive those hours of confusion.

I tried everything: I engrossed myself in work, inventing needless tasks, such as reorganizing stacks of files and redrawing those organizational charts that no one in the ministry was interested in or even remembered; I started to drink occasionally in the evenings, though I stopped when I realized that it made me more tense the following day and less capable of mastering my emotions; and sometimes, after a morning of stealing furtive glances at her from my desk until I felt a viscous fluid begin to rise up in my throat and almost choke me, I would mumble an excuse, hasten out of the office, and walk and walk, rapidly and blindly, veering from one street into the next with no sense of where I was going, until finally I'd succumb to exhaustion and turn into the nearest coffeehouse or drag myself home.

Nothing worked. I certainly had no concentration for reading, which I had long since abandoned as a pastime anyway. Perhaps my sole solace was the appearance of a suitor for Suad, the eldest of my two sisters. He was a teacher and the brother of a friend of hers in the neighborhood. He was not in a position to make financial demands on us because, to be frank, he said, he could not afford a dowry or a trousseau. However, he had been selected as one of the teachers the Ministry of Education would be posting to Sudan and he hoped to take Suad with him so that they could begin to build their life together there. Suad was all for the idea. Still, I would need a sizeable amount of cash. I would have to cover the costs of the engagement and wedding celebrations and I needed an additional sum to give to Suad so she would have some money of her own. I made several trips to the village near the Khayriya Barrages in order to sell a small plot of land that we had inherited from our father. It was a relief to have such things to distract me.

Even so, there was that day when Suad was displaying one of her new dresses to me, and I blurted out, "That color doesn't suit you, Doha."

"Who?" she squealed mirthfully as she spun back to face me. "Is there some other woman here?"

The panic must have been written on my face, because she caught herself and hastened to save me from my embarrassment. "What was that name you just said? She's obviously on your mind." She stepped forward—her eyes were green, like our mother's, from whom she had inherited almost all her features—and kissed me on the forehead. "You've sacrificed so much for us. Soon Samira will find a husband too, God willing. Then you'll be free to turn your attention to that lady whose name's already slipped my mind."

I don't know how I managed to resume my old routine after Suad's wedding and departure for Sudan. But it was precisely when I had to cope again with being face-to-face with Doha at the desk across from mine and had no preoccupations to distract me that the phone rang and I heard Hatem's voice boom cheerily, "Get over here right away."

As I stepped into his office, he beamed. He stood up, came around his desk and embraced me. "Congratulations! Your study grant's been approved. Get ready to fly to Italy!" Seeing that his announcement failed to elicit my enthusiasm, his smile vanished. "You don't seem happy," he said, unable to keep the disappointment out of his voice.

"Hatem, you know why I needed that grant," I said coolly. "As you know, Suad got married and went to Sudan. Fortunately her husband didn't ask for much so I was able to manage."

He threw me an exasperated look and headed back to his desk. "So start planning your other sister's marriage, or your own, man. What's the matter with you? Are you going to spend your whole life waiting for the axe to fall before you start looking for solutions?"

I took a seat in front of his desk and eased into a smile. "You're absolutely right. But, I just don't know how to change. Tell me, Hatem, how should I reform myself and become like you?"

Hatem shrugged and said, "You're spoiled. That's all there is to it."

I laughed.

"I'm not joking," he continued, "As you know, I was one of the worst students in secondary school and university. My father was determined that I should receive a higher education. He packed me off to Cairo where he had arranged for me to live with a cousin of his. That cousin made it very plain that he found me a burden. To make myself scarce most of the day I'd go to your house or to another friend's house to study. My father sent barely enough money to pay for my keep, sometimes less. He was a poor farmer with less than half an acre to his name." He turned to stare out the window toward the Radio and Broadcast Building. A couple of soldiers carrying machine guns were stationed on the rooftop. But his gaze was fixed on something more remote. "You think you have it rough because you have to take care of two sisters, because you barely managed to scrape enough money together to marry off one and now you have to worry about the other. What if I told you that I have eight brothers back in our village and that not one of them has finished primary school or succeeded at work? The ones who went into business failed and the ones who were farmers are now hired hands. If I met all their demands for money every month, I wouldn't have enough left to feed my own family. In fact, I'd have to go into debt."

"Still, you owe them something."

He turned toward me and said, "True. But I've let them know my limits. I deduct a small sum from my salary every month and send it to them. It's much less than the amounts they ask for in their letters. I know it barely makes a dent and I'm filled with shame every time I go back to the village and see the abject poverty they live in—the kind of poverty that means flies crawling around their children's eyes, filthy bare feet with cracked soles, tattered and grimy gallabiyas, faces drawn and sallow from hunger. But what can I do? Either I climb into their boat and sink along with them, or I save myself and watch them drown. You tell me what to do."

I made a stab at lightening his mood. "Have you forgotten, Hatem? I'm the one who came to you for advice."

He nodded morosely and said, "You didn't do me a great favor that day when you saved my life."

"Well, please accept my apologies."

Finally, he laughed. He shook his head as though to clear it and said, "Yes, let's get back to you. I just can't understand this apathy that's come over you—you of all people. In secondary school and university you were so filled with zeal and were all, 'Onward comrades! Put your chest to the bullet! Our lives are yours, dear Egypt!' Now you just bury your head, clock in the office, and go straight home again. Is this how you want to spend the rest of your life until you retire? Tell me, why did you give up politics—and everything else for that matter?"

I looked out the window at a patch of blue sky and caught sight of a kite sailing in the air, its wings steady. I said, "If I knew the reason for this 'apathy that's come over me,' as you put it, I wouldn't be here asking for your advice."

"But I told you what to do. Many times. Come and work with us in the Socialist Union. Why don't you give it a try?"

I shook my head slowly back and forth. "I don't have a talent for giving speeches and holding meetings."

"I think you're afraid of getting your hands dirty. And maybe you would get your hands dirty by coming to work with us. But, my friend, if you keep sitting on your hands, you'll get nowhere."

I remained silent. Hatem sighed and said, "Then, at least try to take advantage of this opportunity to go to Rome. It will give you time to think of a way to make a fresh beginning when you get back. You have to change."

Suddenly he broke into a crafty smile. "Anyway, I have some other news for you. At least this should make you happy. Madame Doha . . . ." He paused to observe me closely, with that smile still pasted on his face. My body stiffened and my heart beat faster, but I fought to keep all emotion from my face. Finally, he resumed, "Madame Doha will be going to Rome with you."

I was stunned. Nevertheless, I forced my face into a mask of blandness. "And why should that make me happy?"

Hatem stabbed his forefinger in my direction and said with the calm assurance of one stating the obvious, "Hey, I know you as well as I know myself. You're head over heels in love with her. There's nothing you can hide from your brother, Hatem."

"You're imagining things and you just want to . . . ."

He cut me off with a wave of his hand. "Okay, we'll drop that subject now. Have you found out who her connection is?"

After a moment's thought he continued, "It must be somebody very high up. Don't look at me that way. If I knew who he was I'd tell you. Anyway, I regret to inform you, my dear friend, that it's not she who is going with you to Rome but you who are going with her."

"What do you mean?"

"I mean that grant was approved for her sake, not yours."

"But why?"

"How should I know? Apparently she has more expertise than you in administrative organization." The room echoed with the ring of his laughter.

Back in the office I asked Doha whether she knew if she had been nominated for a study grant. She smiled and said that if I wished to nominate her she'd have no objection; in fact, she'd be delighted. When I relayed the news I'd just heard from Hatem, she stared at me with open-mouthed disbelief. I observed her closely. Her surprise is genuine, I thought. She'd known nothing of the machinery at work for her.

5

When the ministry's official letter of approval arrived I imagined that it was now just a matter of packing my bags and heading off to the airport. In fact the letter only marked the beginning of a seemingly interminable battle with red tape. First, I had to run around collecting all sorts of certificates, each of which had to be countersigned by two officials. These I had to submit, along with the application form for a travel permit, in an envelope marked "Confidential." The application then wended its way through—I have no idea how many—government agencies (nor was I entitled to inquire which agencies or to try to hasten the process). After what seemed an age of being submerged in that labyrinth, it resurfaced with the words "No Objection" stamped on it and an illegible signature scrawled at the bottom. But it didn't end there. A new memorandum had to be penned off, enclosed in a manila envelop together with the aforesaid documents and the application with the "No Objection" stamp, and submitted for processing through another maze of offices, this time in the ministry itself. When it emerged at the other end with the national eagle seal affixed to it, I had to fill out a second application for a travel permit and send it plodding through the rounds of yet another agency. In addition to the innumerable flights of stairs I had to trudge up and down during those weeks, I must have traversed the length and breadth of Cairo hundreds of times as I ran back and forth between the Military Recruitment Bureau, the Civil Records Bureau, the Ministry of Foreign Affairs, the Tax Authority, and countless other government departments. I appealed to friends and acquaintances to help push things along and, often, I contemplated simply throwing in the towel. Doha, meanwhile, didn't have to budge from her desk; all the paperwork came to her. She was miles ahead of me. I asked her, once, how she did it. "I have friends," she answered with an enigmatic smile.

In the course of one morning's treks, I had to tote my papers to Hatem's office for yet another signature. Sayyid al-Qinawi was inside. He was in military uniform. His skin was much darker and his face gaunter than when I had last seen him. This, together with his closely cropped hair, gave him an eerie appearance. He embraced me warmly, saying, "Thank you, sir. I heard that you didn't forget me and that you submitted the Friday memorandum to the board."

Hatem said, "So, Sayyid, have you learned the value of patience now? The government solved the Friday pay problem in all the ministries, even before your memorandum ever reached a soul."

"But would it have been solved if others hadn't filed complaints? Anyway, I thank God it all turned out right in the end." Sayyid then turned to me and asked, "Did you get my letters from Yemen?"

"No."

"That's too bad. I wrote to you about many important things."

"Maybe that's why they didn't reach me, Sayyid. The censors are very busy right now. This is wartime, as you know."

Hatem nodded solemnly in the direction of Sayyid, "He's one of the heroes of Sirwah. I'm proud of him."

"No sir, they never sent me to Sirwah. I'm stationed in a village that's never made it into the news."

But Hatem had absorbed himself in some paperwork. Sayyid turned to me and continued in a low voice. "I haven't fired a single bullet yet and I doubt the war will even get there. The village is way in the north of the country and I don't think anybody's interested in it. Still, our engineers built a school out of ammunition crates and our doctors treated peasants who had never seen a doctor before in their lives. They have a disease over there that I'd never heard of before: a long kind of worm that lives beneath the skin. Even if you manage to get part of it out, the rest of it goes on living, sucking the life out of your body like a serpent. But I've watched our doctors make a slit into the back of a person's wrist and, when a part of that worm appears, they begin to wind it very slowly around a matchstick and then tape it in place. Every day after that they wind a little more around the matchstick until, after a week or ten days, a tiny black head comes out. Then, before you know it, the blood comes rushing back into the patient's yellowed face and he's walking around again as sturdy as a horse—all without any medicine or surgery or anything. Can you believe it?"

I was disgusted but intrigued. "What's it called, that worm?"

"I asked a doctor who told me some long foreign name, which I immediately forgot." He laughed, but then his eyes widened with a sudden earnestness. "But you know, they don't like us over there. Believe me, they don't like Egyptians and I can't figure out why."

This caught Hatem's attention. He looked up from his work. "God almighty, what's all this about them liking us or not liking us, Sayyid? We're not talking about a romantic relationship, we're talking about war." He thrust his index finger toward Sayyid and added, "Forget all that talk about love and hate. You, Sayyid al-Qinawi, are making the history of our nation in Sirwah."

Sayyid laughed again and said, "Please stop, Mr. Hatem. I told you I didn't go to Sirwah. Are you trying to jinx me? Now, when I get back to Yemen, they're going to transfer me to Sirwah just to make you happy."

"No, so you can make history."

Sayyid frowned and said, "No thanks, Mr. Hatem. Not if it means dying over there in the mountains. You sound just like the people from Moral Guidance." A flash of defiance had come into his eyes. "Look, it's not that I'm afraid to die. We're all going to die someday. But why should I risk my life for them when they don't like us?"

It was me who answered: "Listen, Sayyid, I think I know what Hatem's trying to say. And you do too, even if you don't realize it. Did you know that in ancient times, before the pharaohs, Egypt was made up of many different kingdoms?"

Sayyid nodded keenly. "Sure I do: 'Menes the Unifier of the Two Lands.' We had it in our preparatory school exams. He was from Upper Egypt."

"Exactly. But how did he unify the two lands? Didn't he have to wage war to do it? It took a very long time before we became one country whose people understood and loved one another. I think that what Hatem's trying to say is that we Arabs, right now, are like the Egyptians in the time before Menes. When unity comes, we'll understand and love one another. But for that to happen, we have to fight, just like Menes. And if that doesn't happen, we'll be crushed, one country after the other, just like what happened to the people in Palestine."

Sayyid turned to Hatem and said, indicating me with his thumb, "A man who speaks this well you should take with you to the Socialist Union, sir."

Hatem nodded in my direction with mock deference. "The venerable professor is waiting to receive a gold-embossed invitation before joining us in the struggle to serve the nation."

"Let's stop fooling ourselves, Hatem," I tried to control my irritation. "What do all those meetings and speeches have to do with serving the country? People who really want to serve their country have to take concrete action, and not just sit around and talk."

"Yeah, or fly off to Rome," he said dryly, shooting me a look to caution me against continuing in that vein in front of Sayyid.

"Or work in the tiniest village. But truly for the sake of the country, not just for one's own sake. A little humility is what's called for."

Realizing that the focus of the conversation had shifted, Sayyid asked, "What's this about Rome?" After Hatem told him, he said, "Congratulations, sir. When are you leaving?"

I cast a despairing glance at the documents in my hands. "At the rate this paperwork is going, the Arabs will probably unify first."

"I'd say that it will be much sooner than that as long as you have Madame Doha with you," Hatem volunteered.

"Madame Doha's going with you?" Sayyid asked.

"Yes," I answered, glaring at Hatem.

"God forbid!" Sayyid said, "Even Yemen's better than that!"

Then he stood up and said, "Well, I'd better be off. My leave's very short and I have a million things to do."

After seeing Sayyid to the door, Hatem turned, took several steps toward me and stopped. "Why did you have to speak that way in front of him?"

"And why did you have say what you said?" I countered. I was just as irritated. "Listen Hatem, the guy's an innocent and I like him."

"I like him, too. Do you have a problem with that?"

"Don't mess around with him. He believes every word you say, so stop telling him things you don't really believe."

Hatem came over and took the chair opposite me. His face was so grimly set that it was obvious that he was making a considerable effort to control himself. When he did speak again, it was with a strained evenness. "Listen, I haven't missed the innuendoes and the disapproving looks you've been giving me for some time now. Tell me, have you begun to suspect I'm a crook, that I take bribes or abuse my authority or something?"

"No, of course not! The thought would never even occur to me. If you were any of those things I wouldn't have you as a friend."

His voice sharpened. "Then, what do expect me to do? In a position like mine where I feel as though I'm jumping through hoops every day and am never sure whether I'll still be here the next? I wasn't born rich, I don't have relatives among the

Free Officers, and the head of personnel sends me every paper he's too afraid to sign himself. Don't I have the right to protect myself by joining the organization that they made?"

"But they're playing a dangerous game, Hatem. It could protect you, but it could destroy you, too."

"I'm well aware of the dangers. That's why I play by the rules they made up. That's why I never show approval of Sayyid's impulses; I don't want to sink along with him. I'm having the hardest time, my friend, setting my sail just to stay afloat. Do you have another solution?"

I gave the question some thought, but ventured no comment.

Hatem continued, "If you have any faith in me, then believe me that by working in politics I'm trying to help my family."

Noticing my raised eyebrows, he nodded in affirmation. "I'm not saying that I'm going to use my influence for them—obviously. But if this country succeeds in standing on its own two feet, then the lot of my wretched family will improve along with it. My brothers' children are now getting an education in the new schools that the revolutionary government built in our village. I hope to live to see the day when they grow up; I like to picture them in better jobs than their fathers have and living a more humane and dignified life."

Hatem stood up and returned to the chair behind his desk. He took a moment to collect himself and then emitted a loud laugh. "I'm not the total opportunist you take me for, my friend, at least not a hundred percent. I'm not trying to deceive you, or Sayyid, or anyone; I'm just trying to steer some boats. Now give me the papers you want me to sign."

6

Finally, everything was set. I was off to Rome.

I had expected to catch my first glimpse of Doha's husband at the airport. I arrived long before dawn on that night in early September. The airport was desolate, its lighting brutal. Only a few passengers roamed its vast halls amid hundreds of black-uniformed soldiers.

Doha was there by herself, but she was certain her husband would show up. "He must be on his way." She shifted her purse nervously from hand to hand. "I'm sure he's coming. He left home after midnight. He said that he had a short errand to run and that he'd meet me here afterward." Her eyes seemed to plead with me to somehow make that come true.

It was not long before the loudspeaker announced that our plane was boarding. With every other step we took toward the gate she glanced back over her shoulder.

We didn't speak much during the flight. Doha slept most of the time, or pretended to.

At Rome airport the passport control officer glanced down at our travel documents and barked out, "Egitto!" This was followed by a rapid fire of speech ending in a sneer. To my surprise, Doha answered back in Italian. Whatever she said made him scowl, stamp our passports violently, and hand them back to us without another word. As we left the airport Doha explained. "He said, 'So here we have a couple of those socialist Egyptians who are kicking the Italians out of Egypt.' I said, 'We haven't kicked anyone out. It's just that the Italians in Egypt don't want to live in poverty like us or like they do in Italy."

"When did you become such a revolutionary?" I jested.

She didn't rise to the bait. "I love my country; there's nothing odd about that. No one respects you if you don't love and defend your country."

Not in the mood for that type of discussion, I changed tack. "So how is it that you speak Italian so fluently? I thought you only knew French and English."

She struck a pose of mock hauteur and said, "My good man, I had an Italian governess when I was a child. From the stories she used to tell me I know Rome as well as if I had been here a thousand times. By the way, I brought along guidebooks and maps, so today I'm going to give you a better tour of Rome than any tour guide."

Doha was making an effort to dispel the gloom that had clung to her since we boarded the plane in Cairo. Throughout the taxi ride from the airport into the capital she sustained an animated running commentary on the passing scenery: "Look, that's the statue of da Vinci. . . . That's the Arch of Constantine. . . . No, I'm not sure. I'd better ask the driver. . . . How beautiful that park is! Look at all those pine trees. . . ."

It was hard to tell whether her enthusiasm was real or feigned, but I did know that she was exhausted from the trip, so I let her talk, as I kept a smile fixed on my face and swiveled my attention in the directions she indicated until we reached our destination.

The hotel in which the training institute had booked us was fronted by towering Roman columns. Several white marble statues—copies of ancient originals—presided over the lobby and its plush red Persian carpets. From the ceiling hung a huge round chandelier boasting loops of well-cut crystal. Our rooms were another matter. Mine reminded me of those ancient dilapidated hotel rooms in Alexandria: the smell of desiccated wood, the threadbare carpet, the dresser drawers that had to be pried open with great difficulty to reveal a stained and dusty interior. Exhausted, I simply changed into my pajamas as quickly as I could, climbed into bed, and fell asleep.

It was late afternoon when Doha called my room to wake me up. "Did you come to Europe to sleep, sir? I'll meet you in the lobby in half an hour."

I was sweating profusely. Rome, I had just learned, could be as hot as Cairo. I slipped into a shirt and trousers and went downstairs to wait for Doha. I pushed through the revolving door and stood in front of the hotel entrance. On the street corner was a fountain: an aged, bearded man sculpted in marble, hefting on his shoulders a large jug from which water spewed into the basin below. His pupil-less eyes made him look blind. On the rim of the fountain sat young couples, some licking ice-cream cones, others kissing.

A woman's voice addressed me from behind in Italian. I turned. She was quite young—about eighteen—and very beautiful. Pointing to my mouth I said, "No speak Italian." She took hold of my hand, turned it palm-side up and drew a figure on it with her finger. "Twenty-five dollars," she said in English, after which she drew a plus sign and said, "Cost of hotel room." Just then Doha appeared and laughed. "Already? You don't waste your time!"

I started to mumble an explanation to Doha, but she was speaking to the girl in Italian. They both laughed and then the girl sauntered off.

"I was waiting for you, and then that girl came up, and . . . ."

Doha placed her hand on my shirt pocket and said, "I know. There's no need to explain. But let me give you your first lesson about Rome: don't keep your wallet in your shirt pocket. May I?"

Before I could utter a word, she had slipped my wallet out of my pocket and into her purse. Doha was happy now. She had shed her earlier melancholy, or she had consciously decided to put it behind her. Her face seemed relaxed and cheerful. She was wearing a sheer silk dress with small red and lavender flowers dotting a white background. She had parted her thick black hair along the crown of her head, creating two luxurious masses that tumbled in front of each shoulder and over her chest, in the fashion of ancient Egyptian statues. I, too, was happy as I walked alongside this beauty.

Doha said, "We're going to discover Rome on foot. But first, we're going to have a pizza on Via Veneto, like all respectable tourists."

According to my watch it was 7:00 PM, but it was still full daylight and sunset seemed a long way off. I was amazed. On our way to the Via Veneto, Doha began to pause in front of the display windows to make quick inspections of their blouses, shoes, and handbags. "Would you look at those prices?" She gasped. "How am I ever going afford even the essential gifts? I have a list as long as my arm."

On Via Veneto we selected one of the restaurants with outside seating. The tablecloths were red and we were shaded by a red awning that stretched the full length of the façade. From my place I caught sight of the Italian girl who had spoken to me in front of hotel. She was on the other side of the street, talking to a man with a camera slung over his shoulder. She hooked her arm in his and they walked off together.

We sipped some wine as we waited for our pizzas. That is, I sipped; Doha would pour herself a glass, down the contents in one go, then lower her glass as she reached for the bottle to fill it up again. She became increasingly animated. By her fourth glass her eyes had grown bloodshot and her laughter raucous. I took the bottle from her and set it on the ground next to my chair. She reached across me and pleaded, "Oh no! Please don't do that. Let me drink, as much as I want. We're in Rome now. You don't even know why I drink. Come on, please."

"No. As long as you're with me, you're not going to have more than two glasses. You don't want what happened in Cairo to happen again here, do you?"

She slumped back into her chair and looked at me imploringly. Then she abandoned the effort and said dejectedly, "Okay. You're right." She began eating in silence.

I was about to ask her why she drank, but I checked myself. I thought it wiser to let that subject rest for the present.

Doha made an effort to recover her good spirits as we set off to discover Rome by foot. At the Trevi Fountain, she closed her eyes and threw a coin backward over her shoulder into the water. Others were doing likewise and so did I. She laughed and said, "That's our guarantee for returning to Rome together sometime in the future. So, what wish did you make when you tossed your coin in?"

"Oh, I wished for nothing and for everything."

"Ha! That's you exactly! You're going to come to a bad end."

In Piazza d'Espagna we climbed the long flights of steps rimmed on either side by pots of brightly colored flowers. As we neared the top, Doha was panting and leaning on my shoulder for support. When we arrived at the Egyptian obelisk at the end of our climb, she said between gasps for breath, "Say . . . hello . . . to your . . . great . . . great . . . grandfather."

The early evening sun had turned the obelisk into a crimson-tinged sword, its hilt sunk in the center of a round bed of red, violet, and pink flowers. To me it appeared out of place and lonely at the head of that stairway in that square. I turned to Doha to convey this sensation, but found that she had sat down on one of the steps, like many others. She was shading her eyes with her hand and absently surveying the square down below.

Soon we were on our way again: past more fountains, beneath church domes, past statues in every street. In the distance, I spotted an enormous dark-looking monument with series of tall, arched apertures along its walls like a colonnade. "That's the Coliseum. We're going there tomorrow," Doha said. The sun was beginning to set. We came across a small park and went in; it was festooned with flowers of every sort. They were large, in full-bloom, and fragrant. Doha knew the names of them all. She bent over each flowerbed to examine them and more often than not she would exclaim triumphantly, "I have some just like these at home!" Then she'd look around her and add, "But not as many and not in the middle of so much greenery."

"I thought flowers only blossomed in spring."

"Actually, there are flowers for all seasons."

As we strolled through the park, we came across a small fountain beneath the trees. Thin parallel jets of water sprang from the ground to form fine glistening strings that stretched between two granite beams, the edges of which caught the spray and transformed it into glittering streams of effervescent droplets. As we stood in wonder at this magic, Doha took hold of my hand, her face a rosy glow. "Have you ever seen anything more beautiful than this liquid balcony for the sun to peer over?" Just then the sun set and its last rays cast their dyes on the billowy clouds. At that moment I took hold of Doha's other hand, turned her toward me and kissed her on the lips. She didn't return my kiss. I backed away. She stammered, "It's . . . it's this sunset. It's this place. I'm not going to scold you . . . but . . . ."

My turmoil must have obvious because she rapidly waved her hands before my face as though to dispel it. "Please, don't look so miserable." She patted me on my cheek, jumped to the tips of her toes, and planted a quick kiss on my forehead to console me.

A sudden shower of rain came to my rescue. We hadn't noticed when the first large, warm droplets began to fall, but now they were gushing down, already soaking our clothes. We started to run. The only shelter we could find was a tall tree with a thick trunk and dense canopy. We stood beneath it, facing one another, as intermittent raindrops filtered through the foliage with monotonous plops. In the early evening darkness, Doha looked at me wide-eyed. Strands of her wet hair were clinging to her neck and cheeks.

"What are we going to do?"

"I don't know, but I love you."

She did not respond and silence enfolded us.

Eventually we returned to the street and flagged down a taxi. Doha edged away from me as far as she could and stared out the window with a fixed gaze that took in nothing.

Back at the hotel, after quickly changing my clothes, I paced my room, punching the furniture and muttering to myself. "Yes . . . yes, I love her. What's wrong with that? I love her. Is that a crime?" I charged out of my room and raced upstairs to her floor. The veins in my temples were throbbing. I knocked on her door, and her voice came back to me clearly but with a slight tremble, "Come in."

She was still in the same wet dress. Her rain-soaked hair was in disarray. Thick strands had begun to crimp and curl. She didn't look around as I entered. She stood, legs slightly astride, leaning toward the mirror on the wall, her hands gripping its carved wooden frame. She said, to her reflection, "I was counting. When I reached a certain number I was going to lock the door." Then she turned and stunned me with a radiant smile and sparkling eyes. When she reached her hand toward mine, I took that hand and kissed it. . . .

Her hair, now nearly dry, spread over the pillow in a black silky mesh of tiny interwoven crescents. I gathered them together in my hands and breathed in their fragrance of rain and Doha.

She was crying now. When I asked her whether she felt guilty, she turned her head away.

I said, "I've loved you for so long."

"I know."

"I didn't mean to, but I fell in love with you."

With her face still averted she said, "I know. I could see that. Only this evening I admitted to myself that I love you too."

Then she reached her arms around me and hugged me to her with all her might. Her voice was muffled and taut as she resumed, "Yes, you didn't mean to, and I didn't mean to. But this is what happened. So don't say anything more."

And I wasn't able to say anything more.

But suddenly, Doha flung out her arms and began to shake her head from side to side and laugh. "I'm happy! There's no reason to lie. I'm happy! Happy!"

She continued to laugh softly and shake her head. Her face glowed, even if tears still clung to her cheeks.

7

Doha was cheerful next morning, over breakfast in the hotel dining room. She said, "Do you know what? Once, an old aunt of mine read the grounds in my coffee cup and told me I would spend my honeymoon in Rome."

"Are you going to marry me, Doha? I mean after you . . . ."

She put her hand in front of my mouth. "Shhh. I was engaged at the time and when I related that to my fiancé we decided to fulfill her prophecy. But at the time of our wedding he was too bogged down with work: there was a ministry crisis, or new elections. . . . I don't remember, exactly. So it was two days near the pyramids in the Mena House Hotel. But, you can't really call that a honeymoon, can you?"

"So you will marry me?"

Doha raised her hands in exasperation. "Why are you being so stupid this morning?"

There she sat, in a rose-pink blouse, her lips lightly painted the same color, gesturing animatedly, occasionally sweeping her hair out of her face with her fingers as she spoke in an uninterrupted stream, while I could barely get a word in edgewise. I was still in a dream. I was indeed stupid that morning.

Out in the street, Doha laughed and said, "But what a strange start to a honeymoon: two students off to school."

"But I'll love the institute because thanks to it I found you."

The institute was annexed to the managerial headquarters of a large office supplies firm. It was right in the center of Rome and, we had learned, close enough to the hotel to reach on foot.

"That's good. At least we'll save on transportation expenses," Doha observed. To which I responded, "And I'll get to spend more time with you every morning." Doha shook her head and retorted, "Unless you grow bored as quickly as most men do." I gaped. She laughed again. To her great delight, we discovered that our way to the institute passed through a small park with large beds of flowers interspersed between the trees.

We were received in a small office by a young, blond Italian woman. She shook our hands and introduced herself as Paola. She said that she already knew our names and asked whether we were comfortable in our hotel. She seemed a jovial sort, an impression enhanced by her heavily accented English — the rhythmic stress and her way of drawing out the final syllables. "It's a very simple matter," she said. "If you don't like it we can change it." Before we could answer, she said, "As you know, the course began several days ago. We wrote to you to tell you the exact dates, as I can see from these copies of the letters we sent to you." She paused to look at the carbon copies. "Oh! And this one too. You're not alone; there's another student from Milano who isn't here yet. Do you know Milano, here in Italy?"

Doha and I exchanged knowing smiles as Paola, absorbed with the documents in her hands, gave the top one a disapproving flick with the backs of her fingernails and said sarcastically, though seemingly to herself, "Well, if Milano is so late, then we are grateful to you for coming all the way from Cairo." Then she raised her head as though just recalling a piece of vital information. "Here, as you know, our approach to management is based on liberal economic theory. You, I believe, are from a socialist country."

I immediately felt myself bristle, just as Doha had the previous day. I said, "Yes, we're from a socialist country, but, as you are aware, a branch of your company does a lot of business there. I believe it's the largest branch in all of Africa, isn't it?"

As I spoke, Paola observed me with a look of wonder on her face. When I finished, she erupted into a peal of laughter. "Why are you so serious? Is this your first time in Italy?"

"Yes."

After a brief pause she said, "Soon you'll learn how to take things as they come. Here you'll find socialists, communists, capitalists. They all talk and talk, but nobody means what they say." She nodded to confirm her point, which she reiterated: "Here, nobody means what they say."

Then she turned to Doha and said, "The lectures will be in English. But I think you know Italian."

"How did you know?" Doha asked in amazement.

"Our Cairo office told us."

Suddenly Paola seemed a little nervous. As she led us out of the door, she said, "I'll introduce you to the professors and the rest of the participants before the lecture starts. There are some from Africa and others from Asia. Did I tell you I'm called Paola? Please, if you have any problems, I'm here to solve them."

But we had nothing to complain of in those early days. In those early days we were in love.

Our daily lectures lasted until noon. Even though we sat apart so as not to betray our secret, we'd sometimes exchange glances across the room and, in a flash, read each other's thoughts. I'd feel jealous whenever I overheard Italian men expressing their admiration of Doha's beauty and elegance. But I also felt happy. It was me she loved, I reminded myself.

One afternoon in those early days, we were—merrily, as I recall—making our way to the Coliseum. We had put off that tour for several days. I hadn't been particularly interested, simply because I was content merely to be with Doha wherever we were. But, that day she insisted.

We were walking side-by-side on the pavement when she directed my attention away from her. "Look at that beautiful Italian girl over there. Look! I won't get angry if you look at her."

"Even if I looked I wouldn't see her. You're the only one I see."

"And what about that one who always sits next to you in the institute?"

"The Belgian girl? She's always asking me for translations of English words. Believe me, I don't even remember her name."

"I'll remind you. It's Claire."

But I wasn't lying. In all of Rome, my mind registered no one but Doha.

In the Coliseum, as we tread cautiously over those ancient tawny stones, Doha said, "Beware, we're walking across a sea of martyrs' blood." She chuckled and added, "And the blood of their executioners, too, and of all sorts of savage beasts!"

"Now don't let what I'm about to say upset you," I said lightly, "but I once read somewhere that the blood-thirstiest spectators at these Roman massacres were women."

"That doesn't surprise me one bit, considering all the subjugation and oppression they suffered at the hands of men," she countered. "It probably quenched their thirst for vengeance to watch men being slashed by swords and gnawed at by savage beasts."

She was several stairs ahead of me as we headed up the ranks of spectator seats. She took a seat in one of the upper stalls and I sat down next to her. Far below us were the remains of the oval arena that had soaked up so much blood. Around us were several tourists snapping photos of the broken columns and the crumbling red brick domes that had once housed the executioners and the beasts below the arena floor.

I knew I was about to tread on dangerous ground, but I could not keep myself from asking, "What sort of man is your husband?"

I could feel her stiffen, but she turned to me and answered calmly, "What sort of man is he? Extremely gentle and sensitive. Extremely handsome, too. But like most people who are extremely sensitive, he's also extremely egotistical: he knows how to use his strengths and his weaknesses to his best advantage."

"That's a bit over my head. Perhaps if you put it more simply, I'd understand."

"Was it really that difficult? Okay, I'll explain. You asked me what type of man he is. He's the type who could commit suicide just to spite me. Even worse, he would happily die a natural death if it meant making me suffer."

I said no more, but it was too late. Doha had withdrawn into herself and now spoke more to herself than to me.

"Haven't I seen enough of how men behave? Do you think that after all I've lived through I still don't understand? I was my father's first child. He had wanted one for a long time—a boy, of course. So when I came along, he determined that I'd be better than any boy. Before I was five, I had my own piano teacher and French tutor. When I was a little older, he would take me to the farm and explain to me how crops were cultivated and harvested, and he taught me how to ride a horse. That was before I'd even started school. I was to be his prodigy. He bragged of me to his friends and had me show off my skills at piano, foreign languages, and arithmetic. At the time this pleased me immensely; it made me feel proud and I was an eager partner in his game. I only discovered much later that he had robbed me of a normal childhood and its innocent joys.

"After I finished secondary school at the Lycée des Soeurs he wanted to send me abroad to obtain a university degree. He wasn't sure whether I should study law or medicine or business, and he was wavering between France and America. But one day I surprised him. I told him that I'd fallen in love and that I was going to get married and stay in Egypt. He refused to believe it. He fought my marriage every inch of the way. I think he still refuses to accept it. Do you know that he remarried not long after my wedding? I think that was his way of exacting revenge."

"But you married out of love, didn't you?"

"Of course. How could I not love him? He was the idol of every girl in the country club to which both our families belonged. He was a celebrity: his picture was always in the paper, he spoke at rallies and several years later he would become a minister. Who couldn't fall in love with him? So, yes I loved him; and he told me that he loved me—and maybe he really did. We were very happy during our first months of marriage. But then he began to revert to his old lifestyle. He was used to having women fawn over him and, at the same time, he wanted me to be the beautiful, intelligent housewife he could be proud of: the woman who'd play the perfect hostess at his dinner parties and receptions and who'd rear his children, while he indulged in his playboy lifestyle on the side. Not that his escapades were secret, even then; he didn't even try to hide them. That's when I learned how to drink. It's also when I learned how to spoil his game, and I got so good at it that he stopped hosting dinner parties. Then, after disaster struck, he used his misery and need for me to keep me enslaved. Now do you understand?"

"Yes, I do. Please forgive me for bringing it up."

"Do you think there's ever been a moment when I've forgotten it? Do you really understand? How could you?"

"Maybe I don't understand completely. But I do know that I love you."

"Ha! He loves me!" she scoffed. "What easy words to say."

She now sat as rigid as steel, clasping her knees with her hands. A wave of anxiety swept up inside me as she continued to speak, in a low, biting tone, without looking at me, "And here's another one. Another man who says he loves me. He talks about altruism and feigns innocence, all the while planning to destroy me." She turned her face toward me, eyes narrowed, "Isn't that right? You waited a long time to possess me, isn't that right? You plotted and schemed to humble me to satisfy your pride."

I seized both of her hands in mine. "Doha! None of that's true and you know it. I love you and I want to marry you."

She snatched her hands away. "What an honor! Why should I want to marry you? Who are you anyway? You don't even know the names of flowers."

I stood up. I was desperate. "I don't know what they're called, but I love them. I don't understand you completely, but I love you. Let's leave this place, at least. There's no sense having this conversation here."

Doha shot to her feet. Her face was contorted in anger. "I asked you, who are you? What do you want from me? Haven't you men had your fill of vengeance? What more do you want?"

I stared at her wide-mouthed, at a total loss for words. Then I turned and walked down the stairs. Before leaving, I looked back. She was still standing up there at the top of the crumbling tiers.

I stormed through the streets, furious and insulted. So she wants to break it off now, does she? And why not, if that's what she wants? Because I don't know the names of flowers. Because I'm "another one." I said what was in my heart, but she turned me down. I asked her to marry me and she slapped me in the face.

Where did I go wrong? Come on, don't lie to yourself. You know what your mistake was? What a despicable thing to do: ask a woman who was already married to marry you. Why deny it? There was some truth in everything she said. Part of me was expecting to gain something out of this trip. Didn't Hatem hint as much? Maybe I didn't plan it, but I prayed for it and I seized the chance. Yes, I'm "another one," as she said. Another man, after her father and husband, who wants to harness her to his own ends. But still, there's a difference: I love her. Even so, what kind of torture will I have to endure if we stay together? But loving her as much as I do, what would become of me if she left me?

I trod the pavements aimlessly beneath the glaring sun, although somehow my feet brought me to the hotel. I was exhausted and drenched in sweat. The moment I reached my room I went directly to the bathroom to wash my face, but no sooner had I turned on the tap than I heard a knock on my door.

Doha stood motionless in front of my open door. I too stood frozen, unaware that I should ask her to come inside.

She raised her large eyes to mine and said, "Are you very angry at me?"

"Yes."

"Very, very angry?"

"Yes."

She stepped toward me until her body almost touched mine. Her face was extremely pale. "Then you can't love me very much. What kind of love is that when you can't even protect me from myself?"

I pulled her into the room and shut the door.

Two leather-upholstered chairs faced each other in front of the closed window. She sat in one, I in the other. She fixed her eyes on a darkened spot of the wall behind me; I fixed my eyes on her. Eventually I said, "What's going to happen to us?"

I recalled having heard those words before.

8

oha's fascination with ruins puzzled me. I can understand one being an antiquities buff, applying one's
imagination to ancient stones and engravings to con-
jure up the past to the mind's eye. I can understand visiting a
new city and being as keen to tour its antiquities as to behold
its modern monuments. But Doha's love for antiquities was of
a different order. If I had let her have her way, we would have
spent our entire time trekking between Roman temples, ancient
catacombs, and the remains of amphitheatres. If I suggested we
go to a film, a restaurant, or a nightclub, she would practically
yawn. She would invent some excuse and then placate me with a
compromise solution, which invariably meant her other favorite
places: Rome's parks and gardens. There she would contemplate
the flowers and gaze silently at the trees.

"As beautiful and fragrant as they are, flowers are more than
just color and scent," she'd say. "If you studied each individual
one, you'd discover an entire world that you could live in for
an eternity—were it not, unfortunately, that their lifespan is so
pitifully short. Take these carnations, for example. No two are
exactly alike, that is unless you annihilated their individuality
with a passing glance. Look closely at each flower's flock of
little petals, ornamented in finely variegated hues of red, white,
or pink and sometimes subtle combinations of two colors. Note
the way they fan out to form a rippling fringe of tiny overlapping
semicircles. And each individual petal, is it not a butterfly wing
yearning to flutter delicately before your eyes, waiting only for

your love to give it the breath of life? Give yourself over to that kingdom of butterflies, for once they sense your love, they will draw you to the heart of the flower and become your crown, transforming you into someone more delicate and more beautiful than you are as you share in their ethereal nectar."

And Doha would say, "A tree is not just a cluster of leaves and shade, even if its greenery offers your eyes and heart an oasis in this desert of a world. A tree beckons you to ascend with it toward the sky, but not only with your sense of sight; you must transform yourself into that mysterious essence that ascends through its core, turns to leaf on its branches and takes flight toward the heavens on the verdant wings of palm or oak."

You seemed impatient, almost angry, when you spoke, Doha. Was that because you sensed the awe and bewilderment in my gaze as I tried to follow your communion with the flowers and the trees? But believe me, I was trying to be with you in those flowers and trees. It was all so new to me, but I was trying.

How did I ever manage to keep up with you as you flitted from that fragile dewy world to the aridity of rocks and ruins? I must have heard the history of every stone in Rome. You recounted the stories of the many Egyptian obelisks there: which temples they had originally come from, when they were shipped to Rome, which Caesar had erected them. As we stepped through the remains of Roman arenas and temples you related to me who built them, when they were destroyed by earthquake or fire, and how they were restored. From you I learned the locations of the underground passageways where the first Christians worshiped in secret, then the alterations the Christians made to the Roman temples and how they painted the Virgin Mary over images of Aphrodite or Athena. I had never had the slightest interest in these things before, but somehow you transmitted to me their ancient magic.

When exactly did that begin? Was it after our first argument? Or perhaps a little before then? I don't remember exactly, but it was still in those early weeks at any rate. That day, Doha took me to the ruins of a temple. All that remained were a few severed columns and many empty pedestals that extended in long, even rows along white paving stones whose many cracks exposed the brown earth below. Was it a temple of Dionysus? Or has my mind merely transformed it into a shrine to that god? Perhaps. Doha had brought her guidebooks and she was following the diagrams, not of the ruins that stretched before us, but of the edifice that had once existed. "Here's the god's sarcophagus." She pointed to a spot in the void between two columns, frowning dubiously. She shifted her gaze between the diagrams and the vacant expanse between amputated columns and over the scattered debris of stones in order to ascertain that yes, indeed, the sarcophagus was there. She pointed to another spot. "And there's the statue of the god and the chamber of mysteries." She walked in a straight line toward the spot, counting her paces. When she reached a certain number she turned right and exclaimed jubilantly, "You see? I knew it! Of course it had to be here. How could it not be?" She sculpted an imaginary structure in the air with her hands. "Right here."

"After you cross the threshold, ye supplicant, from the open air and merciless sun into the temple, you proceed along there between those rows of columns which cut the sunlight into strips of shade and transform its scorching blaze into a tranquil glow. Continue further, heart tremulous, as your feet brush this sacred floor, until you reach the roofed hall—over there—where, gradually, you step into an ever-deepening darkness lit only by your devout heart and the flickering wicks of distant candles. Perhaps you only imagine those candles. Perhaps they're not there at all, and you are being drawn to the god by a light that shines from within you. But he is here, for you; in the midst of the heavy darkness of the temple, your god shines and becomes manifest. He accepts your offerings of flowers and vows. He reaches with his firebrand into your humble and adoring heart and—here—in the chamber of mysteries you are baptized and redeemed. Now you leave. No, not from where you entered; from that portal, over there.

"You're outside again. The sun smiles for you; life breathes all around you; nature lays out a magnificent feast. There, on the sacred lake—can you see it?—fleeting flares of sunlight dance across the surface of the water and glance off the leaves in that grove, paving a gilded corridor over your head and beneath your feet. But wait! In the midst of that grove—from over there—a procession is coming your way. Why, it's a procession of priestesses and maiden supplicants in white gossamer gowns. They're drawing closer to you; their dulcimer song wafts over the air, speaking to you, confiding in you alone; and the tinkling of their tiny bells whispers to you, beckoning you to wine and love and merriment. Go now, faithful devotee. The god has imparted his essence in you. You can become one with the trees, the mountains, and the seas. With love, you and he become one; you are the universe, you are the ultimate. Can you see?"

Yes, Doha, I could see; it was impossible not to. You had resurrected the shattered temple before my eyes. Its scattered stones, its severed columns, its cracked and crumbling walls reassembled themselves piece by piece as I drifted with your voice through that corridor between marble columns while a melodious chant hummed softly in the distance and the air filled with a delicate rustling of wings and a fragrant scent.

How could I not see?

As I held you in my arms you murmured, "Can you see, Faust? This is a world of music, not strife; of love, not rebellion. So surrender yourself to it. Do not think."

Yes, Doha. Here I am, ready to be enlightened by your love, with you by my side and inside me. But, when you move away, I'm frightened. Who are you? Which face is yours?

9

Is yours the face I saw that night at the Roman temple? Was that Dionysius who transformed our shabby hotel room that evening into a cradle in which we floated on a wave of love while invisible nymphs summoned us to ceaseless passion? Together we dove into the heart of the wave, letting it carry us as it rose and fell, as it spiraled and pulled us into its vortex and plunged us toward a dark and distant depth inhabited by those nymphs who never tire of singing, as we drove ourselves further and further toward them when suddenly . . . suddenly, just as we were about to touch that depth, our hands clasped together, the wave hurled us to its crest. Our hearts trembled, our bodies heaved, but the wave bore us up again, rocking us gently on its back and spraying us with its fine, refreshing mist as silence descended and we were enveloped in grace . . . until the whispered call from below began anew.

Are you the Doha to whom I was also introduced that night? The Doha who stood before her mirror, barefoot, in a sheer white nightgown, her back to me as I gazed at her from a low chair? The Doha who turned toward me with a flushed and smiling face and asked, "Don't you know me?"

I stood up. I wanted to hold you again, but you fended me off with both arms outstretched, although you were still smiling and your eyes were still gleaming. At that arm's-length you laid one hand on my waist and the other on top of my head, and repeated the same question with an air of surprise that hinted at reproach, "Don't you know me?"

"If only I knew you as much as I love you," I answered.

"But how can that be?" Your tone still held the same per-plexed surprise. "How can you still not know me?" You let your hands drop to your side and said serenely, "Am I not your wife, your mother, and your sister? Do you really not know me?"

You swept your hand gracefully downward to describe the contours of your body; you brought it up to indicate your black hair, gathered loosely to one side and tumbling over your bosom; you pointed at your black eyes accentuated solely by your thick eyelashes and eyebrows. Your movements were so totally sedate, your posture so stately, and your voice and expression so solemn that I felt confused and somewhat apprehensive. You pushed me gently back toward my seat, pulled over the other leather-upholstered chair and sat facing me. You cast your eyes around the small room as though searching for something, although there was nothing there but the ancient wardrobe and a cheap print of a white sailboat on the crest of a billowing blue wave. That gleam was still in your eyes as you shook your head sorrowfully and said, "I can't blame you if you don't know me. I'm not wearing a sign."

I laughed nervously and tried to lighten the atmosphere. "But it's written on your forehead."

You brought your hand up and ran your long, graceful fingers across your forehead as though you believed me. "No, there's nothing there. It wouldn't be there anyway." Suddenly you shivered; you hugged yourself with your naked arms as though a chill wind had swept into the warm room. I stood up, alarmed, and asked, "Doha, what's the matter? Are you ill?" Your face was pale, but you shook your head and said in a low voice, "No, but tonight I feel the same as I did the first night. Come, sit here."

You slid to the side to make space for me. I wrapped you tightly in my arms so that the chair would accommodate us both and I asked, "What first night?"

Your head was buried in my shoulder when you began to speak. "The night when I first learned who I was. I've never told anyone this before, and I don't know why I'm telling you now. Maybe you'll be able to tell me when I finish . . . .

"I was very young when it happened—seven, maybe eight. I was asleep, alone in my bedroom with my favorite doll next to me. My eyes sprang open. I knew someone else was in the room. The window had been left open because the weather was hot. I wasn't the least bit scared. I looked toward the window, but all I could see was that rectangle of night sky, adorned with a sprinkling of stars. But then, into that black patch floated a perfectly full moon. And there he was, as clear as could be in the middle of that moon. I knew immediately the moment I'd opened my eyes that he had left the room and turned into a moon so that I wouldn't recognize him."

"Who was it? Who appeared to you that night?" I asked urgently. I tried to lift your chin so that I could look into your eyes, but your head resisted my hand. You raised a limp arm, placed a finger on my mouth and continued speaking as though I hadn't interrupted.

"At that moment my mother came into the room and flicked on the light. Her eyes were still sleepy, but they peered at me oddly, as though surprised to see me still in bed. 'What was that noise you were making in here?' she asked. When I told her that I had been in bed the whole time, she cast her eyes around the room and said, 'I was sure that . . . but maybe it came from another room.' I wanted to tell her that she was right, that the noise had come from my room. I looked toward the moon, but he wasn't there. I said, 'Mother, I'm Aset.'"

I shot to my feet, nearly pushing her off the chair. "Doha, why are you telling me this now? We were so happy. What are you trying to say? Who is this Aset?"

But she simply sat there, her hands resting on the armrests. A small round ceiling lamp cast a white glow over her head. Her eyes had become blacker and deeper against the pallor of her face, and they seemed to stare not at me, but through me. Her mouth curved into a faint smile as she said, "Aset. Aset whom they now call Isis."

Calmly you signaled me toward a chair. "Sit and don't interrupt me. I told you I've never mentioned this to anyone before you. I have no idea why I'm telling it to you tonight."

Your voice was frail and tired, but it had an edge of authority that would brook no argument. I took the seat facing you as you continued your story in voice that was close to a whisper yet perfectly distinct.

"My mother understood nothing, but that didn't bother me. She was standing there, but she wasn't real. The bed I was in wasn't real. Nor was that room or all the things in it. I knew that I was Aset and that Osiris had made himself visible to me in the moon and promised to take me with him aboard the ship of the gods so that we could set sail across the heavens together. I closed my eyes and fell asleep. I was so happy that night. Osiris had told me his name and taught me mine. He had scolded me for not having known these names before. My nanny at home and my teachers at school had taught me all about Jupiter and Aphrodite, but no one had ever said a word to me about Isis or Osiris. But I also knew that Osiris didn't want me to tell anyone about what had just happened. So I didn't, then I eventually forgot it, or perhaps I imagined that it was all a dream.

"Ten years later, I went to Luxor for the first time with my father. I was in my last year of school. We flew into Luxor at about noon and we stayed at the huge hotel next to the temple. I was tired so I went to bed. But did I really sleep? I tossed and turned; I'd doze off and dream, and wake up to see the images of my dreams suspended in my room. I saw myself in the midst of a marsh. A snake slid through the water, slithering between the tall reeds. I heard a child cry. Did the snake bite him? I cried. Then I saw myself in a boat floating across the sky. Then I was a bird in flight, a kite, circling in the air far above the Nile that coursed through the wilderness. I dove down. On the surface of the water drifted a boat, or a piece of wood, or a crate. I spread my wings over that floating form on the Nile and turned back into a woman. One moment I was sprawled on top of that thing, the next I found myself in the arms of Osiris who had appeared to me as a moon when I was younger. I got out of bed, drenched in sweat. I looked at myself in the mirror. I could barely recognize myself; I was too beautiful to be me.

"I went downstairs and out to the hotel patio. The rows of tables there were mostly filled with foreigners. A waiter approached and asked me what I would like to drink. I gestured toward my surroundings and asked in amazement, 'What are all these people doing here?' I stood up and left. There was a temple overlooking the Nile—I knew that instinctively. I headed toward it without having to ask directions. Only one obelisk stood in front of its high wall; the other was gone. The tip of the one that remained was no longer sheathed in gold or silver as it had been in the past; it wasn't gleaming with the sacred light of Ra. A man standing at the entrance told me that the visiting hours were over. 'What are all those people doing inside?' I asked. He did not understand what I meant. He said that they were the last tour group of the day. I pleaded that I would only stay a short while, that all I wanted to see was the little sanctuary behind the entranceway. It was in ruins. Pieces of wooden scaffolding propped up crumbling bricks. The place was covered with dirt and sand. Severed arms lay on the ground and half-buried heads peered out of layers of dirt.

"I was filled with rage. 'What have you done to the temple?' I shouted. 'What have you done to the temple? Don't you know that this is where the goddess of this holy site appeared? That's why they built her temple here.' I practically dragged the man behind me as I ranted, 'Look, here was the garden; the lotus beds were here and the rose beds here next to them; and over there were the lilies and irises. Right here were the palm trees and the mulberry trees and acacias. The musk bushes were here, bordering the sacred pond on which swam many different colored geese and swans—what happened to the pond? Over here was a marble stairway leading to a hall of pink granite columns; their capitals were lotus flowers sheathed in gold and their bases were carved with intricate designs. Here was the altar and the sarcophagus, and here, the statues of Osiris and Horus.' I didn't mention that the one was my husband and the other my son. I said, 'Here stood Osiris with his golden scepter in hand and there stood Horus whose sapphire eyes gleamed out of the black polished stone. And over there, just before the stairs to the Holy of Holies, was a compartment where they kept incense and perfumes; the priests' white robes and the lutes and flutes of the maiden musicians were in there, too—where has all that gone?'

"The man, a low-ranking civil servant, followed me without uttering a word as I led him amid the scattered piles of stones that had once been assembled to form the now ruined temple. But eventually he spoke. 'You see, over there,' he said, indicating the spot, 'the statue of Isis is still standing.' I barely restrained myself from shouting. 'I know. I know. But come closer. This isn't Aset; it's Isis. This is a Roman woman in Roman dress. This Isis is a foreign invention. Now take a look here: Aset wore a translucent gown, and sometimes a gown made of feathers, but not this robe with its undulating folds. Aset wasn't that filled out, here, and her face didn't have this vulgar prettiness; it had a much greater and a much deeper beauty. There was no need for those spikes of wheat that the foreigners have her holding; her people knew how to make her face radiate her inherent fertility without having to stick plants in her hands. Those spikes of wheat are superfluous.'

"'How do you know these things?' that man in Luxor asked.

"But his question reached me from a distance. He receded, and the visitors and the rest of mankind, and all those fragments of stone and wood receded with him and vanished. I stood alone, totally alone, at the very core of things, watching the beginning of it all. I was in a void of total darkness and silence. Then, in the midst of that darkness, water gathered and the darkness yearned for light, and there was light. The sun of Ra appeared, and the water sparkled in his light, and small islands rose to greet his brilliance. On each island stood a god. I was there, and Osiris was there. Water separated us, but Osiris reached his hand toward me and I reached my hand toward his, and in the primordial haze our islands were joined and we embraced and became one. Then the gods spread their arms, and below their feet the islands expanded and merged, and thus the earth formed amid the surrounding sea. And the gods exhaled and from that breath man was created to populate the earth. When mankind inhabited the earth, the procession of the gods rose to heavens amid rays of light and celestial music. But the gods had left man blind and ignorant, and when Osiris saw them wandering aimlessly on the earth, he took me by the hand and we went down to them. He taught them how to build houses in which to shelter themselves, and I taught them how to cleave the barren soil and turn it green. And when the people saw the fruits of these blessings, they rejoiced and hailed Osiris and myself as rulers of the world for all eternity. It was my brother Set who broke the cycle; he descended to earth and brought back darkness and desolation. How hard I fought after he killed Osiris. After I gathered all of Osiris's scattered limbs, a falcon fluttered its wings in my bowels and emerged. I, too, took flight and I followed it around the world to restore light and justice. The people knew that it was here, on the banks of the Nile, that I had first appeared on earth, so it here that they built my temple. And when I realized the whole truth, I looked around . . . .

And found nothing but ruins. I cried. I left the temple and walked for a long time along the banks of the Nile — my Nile. I sat down beneath a palm tree — my palm tree — and I cried. The sun was setting; my father, Ra, was embarking on his night-time journey on this red ship. Osiris appeared to me again on the ship of the setting sun and confided in me the secret of all that has gone before and all that will come after. He said that thunder would pierce the belly of the heavens so that rain will pour upon the earth, and the seeds will crack open to bring forth flowers. . . . Come."

Aset said, "Come."

Doha said, "Come here."

She reached both her arms out to me. Her face was beautiful, radiant. And she said, "Come here."

I went to her and kneeled before her. She leaned over to enfold me in her arms as I buried my head upon her tender bosom. I inhaled the fragrance of her perfume mingled with a light layer of perspiration. For several moments she stroked my hair and kissed my head. Then she said softly, "Don't despair; I will gather your scattered limbs and you will be whole again."

I whispered, without moving, "No, Aset . . . I'm not Osiris. I'm dismembered on the inside."

She raised my head slightly from her breast and repeated firmly, "I will gather your scattered limbs and you will be whole again." After a brief pause she added, "But don't be hasty and don't ask about the ways of the gods."

I stood up, taking hold of both her arms to lift her to her feet with me; she was as light as air, as though she had lost all her corporeal weight.

We embraced; we stood on an island.

The waves frothed in the haze.

And a falcon flapped its wings.

10

For days afterward I reflected on what Doha told me that night. I don't believe in transmigration of the soul or in reincarnation or such interpretations of her dream. But I was certain that she was not lying to me. In that close, cramped hotel room, she actually felt that she was Isis—or Aset—and that Osiris had appeared to her in the moon and confided in her a secret that remains closed to me. Why not admit it? That night, too, the walls of that room fell away as she spoke and I saw myself among columns with lotus capitals, obelisks sheathed in gold, and palm trees and flowers, and I was a ray from the sun and a wave on the sea. I, too, had stood at the heart of the universe and seen the beginning. Why not admit it?

Yet, after that night, Doha refused to let me so much as allude to what she had told me. The following morning, when I said on our way down to breakfast, "Good morning, Aset," she started and blanched. She pleaded with me not to mention the subject ever again. "Never, never again," she repeated. "I don't know why I went on like that. It's as though I was obeying some command to speak. Please don't bring it up again. Perhaps, someday we'll understand."

That evening, on our way back from the institute, we stopped in the small park halfway to our hotel. Daytime was growing shorter, the sky was leaden and there was a nip in the air, but Doha wanted to sit for a while on that stone bench in the middle of the park. I sat with her. The leaves on the trees had begun to yellow and wither. The flowerbeds had been tilled and furrowed and their dark earth strewn with new seed. We were both worn out from the previous evening and a long day in which the lecturer addressed the connection between Machiavelli and the science of modern management. He said that people misunderstood Machiavelli's maxim, "The ends justify the means." Machiavelli was not inventing a rule for government but rather elucidating the rules that all rulers must apply, regardless of their opinions and intentions. Like a head of state, the lecturer continued, the head of any institution must seek to ensure the stability and success of his 'state.' Any means that promotes this end is justifiable. He then spoke of how directors relayed instructions via what he termed "group leaders," who, he stressed, were not necessarily department managers but rather were the strongest members of staff. "Say for example, workers are planning a strike, which would obstruct a company's operations. A director on his own would probably not learn of this in advance. However, his group leaders would be in a position to keep tabs on such developments and, hence, to inform him in advance of a possible strike. Therefore, a director must always keep group leaders under his control and constantly reward them in order to ensure their continued allegiance."

We'd heard much of the same before in the training course, but this lecture was more direct and more explicit. In the park that day, I asked Doha her opinion of the lecturer. She turned to me, bewildered. "Who?" Then she chuckled and said, "Do you think I give a damn about what they say in there? It all vanishes from my mind the moment I leave the institute."

"I'm sorry, then. You're not interested."

"But, what did he say?" she asked, now curious.

I smiled lamely and tried to make my voice sound light and derisive. "He said that human beings are evil by nature and that they are to be treated on the basis of that premise; that they can always be bought off with money and cowed into submission."

She seemed to think this over for a moment and then said, "Sometimes good can come from evil."

"That's exactly what the lecturer said, but not in the sense that you mean . . . ."

"And how do you know what I mean?"

"Well," I answered cautiously, "at least, I know that you're not referring to the type of evil he is."

"What do you mean by evil?"

"I haven't thought about this before now, but I think I've always hated oppression. The oppression of people by poverty, by intimidation, and, more importantly, by ignorance — for a person to live and die without realizing the knowledge he missed acquiring, the beauty he couldn't appreciate . . . the life that passed him by entirely."

"If these are your beliefs, then why don't you act on them? Why, for example, don't you get involved in politics, like your friend Hatem, so that you can fight for those ideas?"

I bowed my head for a moment then I turned to face her again. "Do you really want to know why?"

"If you feel like telling me."

"Then, I'll tell you the truth — the truth that I've never revealed to Hatem or to anyone else. Of course, you didn't mean anything by mentioning me and Hatem in the same breath. But the fact is that, in a way, he shaped my life. We were schoolmates in secondary school and we were both very active in student demonstrations. We despised every perpetrator of injustice: the British occupation authorities, the king who sold the country out to the British, the pashas who divvied up the spoils with the king and the British, and those who would live it up in Europe while Egypt was under foreign occupation and its people were starving. Perhaps I shouldn't be telling you this, but you asked for the truth. When the revolution came, we rejoiced; we thought that all our dreams had come true: the British would leave and justice would prevail; the people would no longer have to live in squalid, disease-ridden hovels; they would receive an education and ignorance would vanish; modern cities would flourish; there would be parks and people would walk with their heads raised and children wouldn't have to polish other people's shoes and women wouldn't have to beg in the street.

"Instead, we saw the rise of a new class of kings and pashas who wanted to take over the country for which Hatem and I had been ready to sacrifice our lives.

"One day, in the early years of the revolution, Hatem and I were at the university cramming for postgraduate entrance exams. I'd really sweated to prepare myself for those exams, but then I gave it all up. Anyway, Hatem and I got together with some of our old school friends and we decided to stage a demonstration for liberty, like we used to do before the revolution. We marched out of the campus, Hatem supported on the shoulders of peers, shouting the slogans we used to chant in our secondary school and university days—'We'll shed our blood for you, dear Egypt!' 'No to colonialism! No to tyranny!'—to which we added some new ones, such as, 'Down with the rule of the colonels!' We were a couple of thousand, or maybe several hundred. Our plan was simple. We were going to march on the Revolutionary Command Council building, which was near the university, and proclaim our demands, as we used to do at the time of the king, the pashas, and the British. On those occasions—before the revolution—they would sometimes open fire on us. Once, a bullet nicked Hatem's eyebrow. But we took pride in that.

"That day, just after we crossed the bridge to Gezira Island, but well before we reached the Revolutionary Command Council, a squadron of tanks came rumbling up to intercept the invaders. They were followed by army trucks out of which leaped a horde of soldiers wielding truncheons. They swooped down on us. Some students fled back across the bridge to Giza. But not Hatem. The closer the soldiers drew the more stridently he belted out his slogans. Hatem and I were among the students that were carted off that day. I was sitting next to Hatem inside the truck. He whispered urgently into my ear, 'Whatever happens, don't

tell them that we're civil servants. We could get fired.' They took us to an army camp where the truncheons and black boots set to work thrashing and pummeling our bodies. Then they grabbed us one by one: 'Who organized the demonstration?' 'What party incited you to demonstrate?' 'Who's your leader?' Students were sprawled on the ground, groaning, blood oozing from the wounds on their heads and faces. But not one breathed a word. I took all that in as I waited my turn. My face poured with sweat and my hands, my whole body trembled. Why was it that a bullet hadn't frightened me, but the sight of those khaki belts and black boots lashing and kicking had me quivering in terror? Why did such a mundane thought keep spinning around in my head at that moment: that they'd find out where I worked and have me fired, leaving Souad and Samira to starve and me homeless? What made me commit that act for which I will never forgive myself? Did I imagine that it would spare me?

"I was standing next to a taciturn young officer whose task was to guard us and, when ordered, hand us over one-by-one to his senior, who supervised the beatings. I took that officer to one side and whispered to him, 'I'll confess. The ones who organized the demonstration are that one . . . and that one . . . and that one.' Hatem was one of the ones I pointed to. The officer whispered back, 'Why did you betray your friends? Why didn't you keep silent like the others? If you'd held out for a bit, they would have let you go.' When they started to beat me, I didn't say anything. I didn't confess. But I never forgave myself for that moment of weakness. I've never told Hatem about that incident. But that was when I knew that I wasn't mature enough to get involved in politics. Why not admit it?

"Long afterward, after the evacuation of the British, Hatem tried to persuade me to join the Liberation Rally Organization. 'By working with the revolutionary order we'll be able to achieve what we failed to achieve outside it,' he said. I refused. Some of our dreams had, indeed, been realized: the British had

gone, new schools were being built, and new factories were cropping up everywhere. But I told him that it was none of my concern and that I wasn't old enough to get involved."

I fell silent. I was shivering from the cold as I sat there next to Doha on the stone bench in the park. But I didn't suggest that we leave; I was inert.

Doha also remained silent. But after a while she said, "I believe you. When you betray one person, you betray everything and everyone."

"What do you mean?"

"I mean that when you betrayed your friend, you betrayed your dreams and your principles. You could never be the person you were before."

Then she added calmly, "We're both traitors."

"Please don't say that," I protested. "Yes, we're both traitors, but we can atone. I've told you over and over that I want to marry you, haven't I? It's senseless for you to stay with someone you don't love. Redemption is possible."

"Why did we have to meet? Why did we have to work in the same office? Why did I have to fall in love you? Why did we have to come to Rome together?" Her voice was barely audible, as though she were speaking to herself. "I wasn't interested in you at first. I observed you; I noted your sullen silences, the bewilderment in your eyes, your nervous mannerisms as you tried to impress me with your erudition. And I thought, here's another one, just like the others. Yet, perhaps even then I loved you; suddenly your face would appear to me while I was combing my hair in the mirror or reading a book. I'd feel irritated with myself; my husband was the only man I had ever known. Yet in those moments of anger, I'd have a sudden urge to betray him, because he betrays me all the time, but that was just the anger talking. I knew deep down that I would never do that. Not for his sake but for mine. Not so much out of respect for him but out of respect for myself. Yet on those few nights when my husband

stayed home, I began to imagine you next to me . . . instead of him . . . and I'd feel so ashamed—as ashamed as if I'd actually betrayed him—and I'd fill with an enormous rage."

I repeated, "Redemption is possible, Doha. It was never my intention to love you. I just did. That's all there is to it."

She grasped my hand and said, "Who knows? Who knows why we met and where all this anger will lead to?"

"Why do you speak of anger, Doha? Wasn't it you who said that life should be music, not strife?"

"That's the life I dream of," she replied calmly.

Silence descended. An orange sun sat frigidly beneath dark clouds. Suddenly a light gust of wind assembled the withered leaves into a long, rustling stream that coursed rapidly over the ground, swept upward in a spiraling tail, and then tumbled down to earth.

11

Enter a man and woman. Both are nude. The man is slender, blond, handsome; he holds a whip. The woman is young and beautiful; her long, golden hair flows down her naked back. The man circles the woman menacingly. She tries to escape with lissome dance-like movements. He checks her with cracks of the whip. She falls to her knees before him; she writhes at his feet; she grasps his finely toned muscular calves and pleads. Suddenly the stage turns red. Another naked woman appears; she has long black hair and wields a sword. She thrusts the sword at the man, who leaps backward in alarm and vanishes into the wings. She drops her sword and bends over the woman lying prostrate on the ground. She hugs her and lifts her to her feet. They clasp each other in a long, slow embrace, stroking each other sensuously. The curtain slowly falls to polite, tentative applause.

As the subdued houselights came on, I turned and looked at Paola quizzically.

"Why are you smiling like that?" she asked.

"I'm sorry. But wouldn't you say that the audience here is excessively well-behaved given that they were watching . . . ."

She cut me short, saying somewhat boastfully, "This is the most fashionable nightclub in Rome."

I cast a look around me. The men, hair carefully coifed, wore dark formal suits over brilliantly white shirts with stiff, high collars. The women were in sleeveless, very décolleté evening gowns. A heady blend of expensive perfumes pervaded the room. People were seated around dining tables clad in white linen and on which sat silver champagne buckets, from which peeked the necks of the bottles, wrapped in serviettes. Paola and I were among the few who were drinking only wine. Red and yellow beams from revolving spotlights pierced the smoke-filled darkness.

Paola looked at me with a twinkle in her brown eyes. "I've noticed that you and Doha are always talking about fountains, temples, and statues. I just wanted to let you know that Rome is not a museum and that the people here are alive. Why didn't Doha come?"

"She wanted to, but I think she's a bit worn out."

Paola nodded and said, without conviction, "Really?"

She raised her wineglass to her lips as she surveyed the room. She focused on the women, in particular, while commenting in a low, confiding voice. She would say, "You see that woman, over there? She's the wife of Mr. ___, but she's the lover of the man she's dancing with." I wanted to tell her that the names she mentioned weren't familiar to me, but she prattled on as though those personalities were known the world over. I listened to her with a smile fixed on my face, all the while wondering anxiously whether I had enough cash on me to pay our bill in the most fashionable nightclub in Rome.

In the few weeks since our training course began Paola had made a point of showing up regularly during breaks in order to engage each of the students, in turn, in a friendly chat. Doha was one of the few women in the course and an odd relationship developed between her and Paola. Sometimes, as Paola recounted one of her jokes or made idle pleasantries, Doha would settle on her a long-lashed vapid stare, throwing Paola off form and causing her to stammer to a halt. At other times, they'd huddle together and chatter away in Italian, as though confiding in one another their deepest secrets. When I asked Doha what they'd been talking about — my Italian being virtually nonexistent — she would answer curtly, "I was just consulting her about some things I have to buy." That day, when Paola insisted on inviting us to "an evening out," Doha accepted. In fact, after lectures were over, I discovered that she and Paola had left the institute together. But later that evening, Doha phoned my room to tell me in a strained voice that she was tired and that I should go alone. "If you're not feeling well, I'll stay here with you," I offered. She replied impatiently, "No, you have to go. We promised Paola that we'd come. She's already made reservations, so at least one of us has to be there." "What are you up to, Doha? Are you trying to set me up with Paola? All right then, I'll go." I slammed down the receiver. I had acclimatized to Doha's recent moodiness and evasiveness around me, but her insistence that I go out with Paola set me off. I had begun to sense that she wanted to break off our relationship.

Light music had been playing in the nightclub, but the volume increased as drums and cymbals sounded in.

"Would you care to dance?" Paola asked.

"Very much, but I don't know how."

"Are there many like you in Egypt who don't know how to dance?"

"Yes, I think so. Not that many people dance."

"How about Doha? Does she dance?"

"Perhaps. I really don't know. I've never asked her."

"I'd be very surprised if she didn't. She has a body that was made for dancing: as graceful as the female dancers I've seen in the wall paintings in your ancient temples. You're very lucky."

I felt my neck prickle. Keeping my voice as nonchalant as I could, I asked, "And what makes me so lucky?"

"Because you're with Doha all the time," she said, eyes widened in affected innocence. She giggled and added, "I know at least five in the institute who've fallen hopelessly in love with her."

I felt a sudden clench of panic. "And which five are those?" I asked, struggling to keep my voice casual.

Paola burst out laughing. When I failed to share in her mirth, she, too, fell silent and began to sip at her wine. When the dancing ended, the revolving red and yellow spotlights dimmed and another performance began on the little stage.

A young woman enters a bedroom. She is wearing a sheer nightgown ensemble. She goes up to a mirror and slowly removes these garments to the accompaniment of intermittent strains of sinuous music. A loud drumbeat heralds the removal of each successive item. As soon as she sheds the last article of clothing, she turns toward audience and begins to run her hands over every part of her body. The audience is now treated to a novelty. Having ascertained that all her body parts are where they should be, she embraces an imaginary figure. She writhes tortuously and groans in time with the music, until finally she flings herself onto the bed. The applause was slightly louder this time and there were even a few appreciative hoots and chortles.

When the red and yellow spots began to revolve around the room again, the tables, too, seemed to shift and I felt my head begin to spin slightly. Paola was in a crimson gown and her silky blond hair had been swept upward to form a halo, leaving her graceful, white neck exposed.

"You're beautiful, Paola."

She smiled, applauded theatrically, and said, "Bravo! The gentleman has awoken again and he speaks. This calls for another bottle!" I doubted that I could handle much more wine.

Nodding toward the people in the room around us, Paola asked, "Which one do you like best? Here are the most beautiful women in Rome." Her speech, too, was a bit slurred.

I laughed and said, "You."

"Of course I'm the most beautiful woman in the world," she said with mock disdain. "I meant, which one here apart from me do you like best?"

"Every single one," I jested.

"How very oriental of you."

"And what do you know of the Orient?"

"Quite a bit. We get a lot of easterners in our course. Each and every one of them thinks that every Italian woman has been waiting just for him. Unfortunately, my friend, the fact is that this applies solely to the women on the Via Veneto and other notorious sidewalks." Then she added, with a giggle, "But the reverse does apply. I mean Italian men are very fond of eastern women; they're very fond of Doha, for example."

"That's enough about Doha," I said, none too calmly.

"All right then, let's talk about you. Let's say you're not very oriental." She placed her hand on mine. "Let's say that I love you." She raised her palm in front of my face as though to caution me. "I mean, that I like you." Then she performed that gesture, typical of Italian women, of waving her hand quickly back and forth, as though erasing a blackboard. "I mean, this question of emotions . . . pardon me, signore . . . but this business of emotions ended a long time ago. I mean, I'm very sorry."

"But I wasn't talking about emotions."

She set down her glass and said, without looking at me, "Exactly. And that's why I said I like you. You seem to me a very rational person, quite different from many others I've met. Which is why I'm going to ask you, do you like what's happening in Egypt?"

I set down my glass and attempted to focus what little concentration the wine had left me. "What are you talking about? What's happening in Egypt?"

She shrugged as though it was all so obvious. "You know, taking away people's money, expelling the Europeans and the Jews, the war with Israel—that kind of thing."

The effects of wine suddenly receded to only a slight heaviness of my tongue. I was alert now. "Okay, Paola, let's take these things one by one. It seems that you've heard a lot but know considerably less. In the first place, they are not 'taking away people's money,' as you put it. Here, you have what you term the 'just redistribution of wealth,' which you implement through taxes, isn't that so?"

"But, taxes are not at all the same thing," she protested.

"How so?"

"I mean, they're different. But okay, let's drop that one. Israel—why do you fight Israel?"

I burst out laughing. "We're fighting Israel? When have we ever attacked Israel? Just to remind you, it's Israel that attacked us, together with the British and French, in case you've forgotten."

"But don't you understand why? That's because you want to drive them into the sea. Why do you hate the Jews? Didn't they suffer enough in the war?"

I paused briefly, then asked, "Are you Jewish?"

She drew at her necklace and extracted a large gold cross from its hiding place beneath her cleavage. "I'm very Catholic," she said jovially. "On Sunday I'm going to confess to the priest every detail of this evening."

"Why did you say that? What makes you think we hate them? While you here in Europe were massacring Jews, they lived among us as ordinary people; in fact, often as above-average citizens: many had enormous fortunes and no small number ranked as pashas and served as ministers. But after Israel was created, many of these citizens moved there, taking considerable amounts of money with them, and then they made war on us. Those ones I do hate. But I don't hate them because they're Jewish. I haven't known many Jews, but there was one who was among my best friends. His name was Ibrahim. He refused to go to Israel. He said, 'I'm an Egyptian, and I'm a Jew. I'm going to stay in Egypt even if they draft me into the army. I'll fight, but I won't change my nationality and I won't change my religion.'"

Paola frowned and said, "What happened to him? They threw him in prison, didn't they?"

"Nothing of the sort. He was an employee in a major firm in downtown Cairo. He worked there until he died two years ago."

"You see?" she exclaimed triumphantly.

"See what?"

"He died!"

I couldn't believe this. "Yes, he died. He died like everybody dies: he contracted an illness and died of that. His death shook me deeply. I took part in his funeral procession. He was buried in the Jewish cemetery alongside his father and other relatives. Is there anything wrong with that?"

Paola pressed her lips together and shook her head dubiously. "Still, there's something symbolic in his death."

"And what might it symbolize, please?"

"But it's perfectly obvious. He died because he was psychologically torn and couldn't find peace."

"How would he have found peace?"

"For example, by knowing that there was no animosity between his country and Egypt. If there'd been peace, your friend would have remained alive."

"Even when riddled with cancer, which was the cause of his death?"

She dismissed that with a flick of the wrist and continued, "Take what I'm saying metaphorically. If there were peace. . . . That's to say, if you, in Egypt, I mean, you don't know what a real war is like. We in Europe have lived through such a war. I remember that when I was I child I had to stand in line for hours for a piece of bread the size of my palm. I never knew the taste of chocolate or cookies before I was at least ten. Nobody wants war. Believe me, there are many Egyptians who want peace."

A bell went off in my head. I'd heard these words before, but where? *We in Europe know what real war is like; you don't. Peace is beautiful. Many Egyptians want peace.* "Keep going, Paola."

I had almost barked the command, but no one had noticed. The room was buzzing with loud conversations punctuated by shrieks of women's laughter. The general din overpowered the music, but the band kept playing anyway. Paola, however, looked alarmed. "Go on," I growled. "Some Egyptians want peace. There's an organization working to bring peace. This organization falls under NATO, and so on. Is that right?"

Now I remembered where I had heard it all before. It was on the radio: the confessions of a spy who related how he was recruited. That's why it sounded so familiar.

"Maybe," Paola said weakly.

"No, not maybe. Certainly. So, how many dollars a month? How many dollars will I get a month? How much am I worth to you, exactly? You didn't have to go through all that foreplay: you like me; I'm intelligent; I'm different from all the others. You didn't even have to bother with this night out. Come on now, tell me. How much do I get a month?"

She stared at me morosely for a moment. Then her head jerked back as she erupted into a full-throated laugh. "Not a single dollar!"

"But why? I'm no worse than others."

Still laughing, she said, "You're a lot worse. Your kind is useless. You'd bring me down along with you."

She abruptly turned serious and made a cutting motion with her hand. "It's over. Let's just say that we played our cards and I lost. I wasn't clever enough, or you were the better player. Whatever. I lost. But because you're a gentleman you won't rub my defeat in my face, right?"

So saying, she took hold of my hand and pulled me to my feet. "Come on, let's dance. Now, don't say you don't know how. All you have to do is make like a monkey. That's what they call dancing."

As I held her and we weaved as best we could among the other dancing couples, she giggled. "Still, my friend, you don't have to overdo the monkey bit. There's no need to swing your arms so wildly. Move a little more slowly."

But I stopped abruptly and said, "Listen, did you speak with Doha about . . . about what you said to me?"

"No," she said as she maneuvered me back to dancing. "Doha's obsessed with love. It would be useless to speak to her about anything else."

Ah, another trap, I thought. I asked her, as though the subject were of little consequence, "How would you know?"

"My friend, there's a law of nature that you should be aware of. Every woman must confide her secrets in another woman. I'm talking about secrets regarding men."

"Really? And what did she tell you?"

"Many things. It could be, if you're nice to me, that I'll let you in on some of these secrets myself, tonight."

I led her off the dance floor, bumping into several dancing couples along the way and apologizing profusely. As we approached our table I said, "I can see that you're very confident, Paola. Brazen, almost, like certain women on Via Veneto, though I don't believe I've encountered you there."

"Don't be rude."

But she wasn't angry when she said that. She pressed her body close to mine. "Don't let this go to your head, my friend, but there's another law of nature you should know. The other woman's man is particularly desirable, especially if she's beautiful." She laughed, leaned in closer, and gave me a long, drunken kiss. This, too, caught no one's attention; long, drunken kisses were being exchanged by many couples in the club that night.

I could not help but to fall into the swing of things. We took our seats and I joined in her laughter, but I did not drop my guard: I was not about to let this Italian woman lure me into any admissions. I jested, "This wine's adulterated."

"How about you? Are you adulterated?"

"You'll never know."

With her characteristic dismissive flick of the wrist, she said, "It doesn't matter. You're a very proud man, my friend. I have a trustworthy friend if you want to . . . you know . . . tonight. It's not a big deal, believe me. I just thought that given the state Doha's in tonight. . . ."

"What state?"

Her mouth twisted into a sneer. "What state, he says! Il signor asks me what state! Listen, I can't stand people who play stupid or who play me for stupid. The state you put her in, sir! The state of needing an abortion!"

Suddenly she crumbled in her chair, and she went pale. "I'm sorry," she said gravely. "Doha will never forgive me. I'll never forgive myself." She covered her face with her hands and said, "This wine . . . ."

What happened next is a blur. I have no recollection of leaving Paola. I do recall being back in my hotel room with my phone to my ear, listening to the ringing of Doha's phone. I remember bounding up the stairs and pounding on her door. Still no answer. Then I recall saying, "Doha. Open the door. Paola told me everything. Open the door, or I'll get the key from downstairs."

The neighboring door flung open. A man peered out and growled, "What's all this noise? It's nearly dawn. Are you crazy?"

I lunged at him. He ducked back into his room and swore at me before slamming the door. At that moment, Doha cracked open hers. She was in her nightgown. Her eyes were rimmed with dark circles. She leaned her body against the edge of the door to prevent it from opening further. "Please, leave me alone tonight."

When I moved to push my way in, she thrust out an arm to shove me a way. I stumbled backward and nearly fell.

"Go away. It wasn't you," she hissed.

She shut the door and clicked the lock.

12

I've been disappointed in love before. There was a girl who didn't reciprocate my feelings. Two other relationships fell apart halfway through. I've experienced the pain of rejection, the stings to my pride and self-esteem, and the helpless enthrallment to the cause of these agonies. Against all the hard evidence, I sustained the perpetual hope that, by some miracle, the tree that rotted and crashed to earth would bloom again. There will be a letter or a phone call, I would think, and the face that had left me stranded so abruptly will reappear; her eyes will smile again, our hands will intertwine, and everything will resume exactly as it was. Surely, I imagined, the morning will make those nighttime dreams come true. But over time, as I clung to the fantasies that refused to materialize, I cannot say that the wounds healed, but somehow I learned to live with that sense of battered freedom that became so much a part of me, until a new love came along, and with it another cycle of pain.

But with Doha it was different. The following morning brought me a new Doha: a pale Doha with a stranger's smile. She shook my hand as though we had only just been introduced. Her voice was perfectly calm and ordinary; indeed, almost friendly. She could have been speaking to a good colleague or an old school chum, not with great warmth, but as though she had bumped into him after many years. Whenever I attempted to bring up what had happened the previous night, and what we had between us before then, she cut me short. When, in the grip of desperation as we sat in our small park on the way to the institute, I clutched her in my arms and said, "Doha, why don't you tell me what's wrong? Doha, aren't we lovers? Haven't we agreed to get married?" she did not resist. You did not resist, Doha, as I held you to me. You did not resist as I shook your shoulders demanding answers to my questions. But when my shouting subsided, you backed away a little; lifted your large, black eyes toward mine and regarded me blankly; and with absolute composure and without raising your voice in the slightest, you said curtly, "No. We're not lovers. Not now. It's over. It's best you forget about it."

"But why?"

You gripped my arms gently and said, in the same factual tone, "One doesn't ask people why they fell in love, or why their love died."

Then you turned your attention to the park. You had finished with me, consigned me to the past. You leaned forward and said, "Look, the dahlias have budded. I wonder whether we'll see them flower before we go back to Cairo."

My voice came out thin and unfamiliar. "Is it because I don't know the names of flowers?"

You sat up with a jolt and turned to me in surprise. A smile played on your lips, but you did not reply.

No, I had experienced nothing like that before. What little I had learned of love before Doha was of no avail. Yes, perhaps I felt those initial familiar symptoms: the hope that this was just another quarrel, a temporary alienation that would end with a knock on my door and me taking her in my arms, or by her opening her door when I knocked and her arms reaching out to me. But we no longer even met. In the morning, she deliberately left the hotel well before or after she knew I would. In the institute she occupied her customary place, far away on the other side of the classroom among other people. In the evening, she'd go out with Paola or, quite simply, vanish.

I spent an entire evening writing a letter: *My dearest Doha, my dearest Aset.* I crossed this out and sufficed with:

Doha/Aset,

You promised, Aset, to make me whole again. I've been dismembered, laid to waste. My limbs are scattered and fragmented. I need you. My end is near. I need your breath to revive the spirit of life you had bestowed upon me in the beginning. . . .

I wrote pages. Shortly before dawn I slipped the letter beneath your door. In the morning, I felt myself tremble as the receptionist handed me an envelope with your handwriting on it. My hands fumbled as I tried to open it. When I finally succeeded, I found nothing but my letter to you.

What followed was madness. I recall a night when I pounded on your door and your voice snapped back from the other side, "If you don't go away I'll call the receptionist. And if that doesn't work I'll call the police." Then there was the night when I rang your room; when you picked up the phone I said, "Doha?" But my voice caught in my throat. You calmly replaced the receiver.

I remember phoning again another night. "You whore! Who are sleeping with now? How many guys in the institute are you fucking?" Again you hung up without a word.

Perhaps it was that evening that I went out, picked up the first woman on the sidewalk who said, "Buona sera," and accompanied her to some hotel. She demanded payment before we went up to the room. She started to take off her clothes as soon as she shut the door. I stopped her. I took her by the hand, sat her on the edge of the bed in that tiny room with the dismal brown wallpaper, and pulled up the only available chair so as to sit facing her. "Tell me, please," I asked, "why does a woman leave a man she loves? Why would she do that if she said she loved him and if he knew she loved him?"

She had gray eyes and wore a huge blond wig. She spoke a heavily accented broken English. "Ah! So you're the kind who like to talk?" She laughed and propped her elbow on the short bed frame. "You got twenty minutes. You do what you like."

I spoke rapidly as she watched, screwing up her eyes at times, smiling at others. Finally, she glanced at her watch and said, "Sorry, I told you, signor, I don't know English good. I do not understand everything you say." She pulled up the hem of her skirt, which barely reached midway down her thigh, reached out to me with a smile, and pulled me toward her. "But, I know that in your state, what you need is to sleep with signora Angela. I'm Angela, capito? I'm an angel." She let go of me and fluttered her arms like wings. Then she reached out again and pulled my head to her breast and said, "Come to Angela. Come to mama." I pulled free and rushed to the door. As I stumbled into the corridor, she called out, "Wait! I give you back half your money, if you want."

I recall going to Paola. I left midway through a lecture and went to see her in her office. She was alone. She removed her glasses and set aside the papers she was reading. "Ah, signor. Do we have problems? We've missed a lot of lectures lately."

I took a seat in front of her desk, which faced spacious glassed-in balconies on all sides.

"I'm not feeling right," I said.

She smiled and said, "If you have problems at the institute or with your hotel I can help. As for other problems, I'm very sorry." But she came out from behind her desk and sat in the chair facing me. "Are they very serious problems?"

I burst out, "What did Doha tell you? What did she say about me?"

Paola shot a wary look toward the door as though afraid someone might walk in. Keeping her voice low, she said, "Do you think this is the right place to speak of this problem?"

"I'll meet you tonight, then."

"I'm sorry. These days . . . as you know, the course is about to end and I'm very busy." She fell silent for a moment, then reached out and patted my hand. "You'll make it through this on your own," she said sympathetically. "This is the type of problem that no one can help you with."

"Then Doha did tell you something!"

She shook her head. "No. About this latest problem, Doha said nothing. Believe me, she didn't tell me a word. But I understand." But she was unable to suppress a high-pitched titter. "It's as clear as daylight." She reached out with her finger and drew a circle around my forehead. "Listen, my friend. There was a glow here and now it's gone. I could see that for myself without Doha having to tell me."

"Is that why you don't want to meet me tonight?"

She rose and said, as she returned to her seat behind her desk, "Yes. For that reason and another. Yes, now you, too, are ordinary—just like the others."

I stood and approached her desk. Keeping my voice low I said, "Listen, Paola, I give you my word of honor that this will remain between you and me. I won't tell a soul, but I have to understand. Did you approach Doha like you approached me the other night? Did you speak with her about peace and Israel and NATO and those things?"

Paola rose half out of her chair. Her eyes blazed, and her mouth was formed as though about to hurl a curse. But she regained control and sat down again. Forcing a smile and a carefree voice, she said, "You gave me your word as a man not to bring that matter up again. But listen, since it means so much to you, I'll let you in on a secret: we don't try twice in the same term. We know that you might let something slip if you accepted. Believe it or not, no one approached Doha. Are you happy now? Can this be the very, very last time we bring up that subject? Now you can kindly return to your lecture. I have work to finish."

But I didn't return to the lecture. I went outside and roamed the streets, as had become my habit lately. I entered a small park; the many trees seemed taller now that they were barren of leaves.

I sat on a wooden bench next to an old man. He was working his jaw in a constant ruminating movement that sucked in his sagging cheeks and forced out his tightly pressed lips.

"Do you have a cigarette?" he asked.

I gave him one, which he contemplated as he rolled it around in his fingers before putting it in his mouth and lighting it. On the exhale he said, "This is a rough life, sir."

"Hah! Harder than you think, signor. Have you ever thought of committing suicide?

"Thought of suicide? I've tried three times!" He pulled back the sleeve of his threadbare jacket and showed me his wrist, which was notched with deep pale scars. "This was one time."

"But why?"

He chewed his lips a moment. "Let me see if I can remember."

He inhaled deeply from his cigarette and shook his head. But then it came to him. "Yes, yes . . . I think that one was after my wife died, or maybe that was the time during the war. Another time I jumped into the river, but they always fish you out. They never leave you in peace."

I laughed, but he didn't; his Adam's apple was bobbing rapidly up and down his flaccid neck as he shook his head back and forth. "Signor, when you decide to commit suicide you're already dead. What they rescue is not you, but your corpse."

Even so, I did not commit suicide. But I would go out at night, and walk and walk in the freezing cold, heedless of the nagging cough that was growing worse by the day, until I awoke one morning and found that I was unable to get out of bed. Everything was a blur. When I tried to clear my eyes I found my face drenched in sweat. I could hear myself wheeze. I was murmuring, "Doha." And Doha came. And she was Aset: radiant, black hair loosely flowing, in a long white diaphanous gown, she held a lotus flower; she bent over me, kissed me and brought the lotus flower to my face; and she said, "You will be the flower and when you revive you will not recall the pain." I immersed my face in the deep, wide cup of the flower, and Aset embraced me and we were one: me, Doha, and the flower. Paola appeared; she was furious and shouted, "This is not Dante Alighieri!" My mother came, carrying a slaughtered hen and weeping; then my father, dressed in black, stepped forward and said, "Arrivederci." The flower was deep, its cup bottomless. But Doha did not come.

When I emerged from my bedroom two days later, I was amputated, incomplete. But the remnants resembled me well enough that no one noticed the difference.

13

On our return flight to Cairo I cast my mind back to our flight to Rome a few months earlier. Then, too, we talked little. Like then, we acted as though we were two polite strangers thrown together in adjacent seats. Occasionally Doha drew my attention to some odd cloud formations over which we were flying, or to specks of islands in the sea. "Would you mind?" she said when asking to glance at my newspaper; "Thank you," when I handed over a cup of coffee from the hostess; "Sorry to disturb you," because she had to stand up in order to get something out of her purse in the overhead luggage compartment—that was the extent of her conversation. I, too, barely said a word throughout the trip.

We arrived in Cairo in the evening. Doha made numerous purchases from the duty free store, deliberating at length over ties. By the time we headed to the exit, she was carrying several shopping bags. On the other side of the barrier, in the arrivals hall, I spotted my younger sister, Samira, and Hatem. With them was a tall, elegant man whom I didn't recognize. They waved to us excitedly.

The third person, I realized, must be Doha's husband. I felt her tense up when she caught sight of him. As we emerged in the arrivals hall, he strode toward Doha, arms wide for an embrace. She seemed to recoil; perhaps she even took a step backward. But suddenly she dropped her bags and rushed forward, allowing him to enfold her in his arms as she pressed her face against his broad chest. My sister, at this time, was hugging me while

97

Hatem laughed loudly and bellowed his welcome-backs. When my sister finally released me, Hatem grasped my hand and pumped it energetically. At one point he exclaimed, "What's this? Don't they have food in Rome? You've grown so thin!"

I aimed for wit: "I caught the European flu. Watch out or I'll give it to you!"

Another hand was proffered. Doha introduced its owner: "My husband, Shukri." After which she turned to greet Samira and Hatem. I shook the hand and met a friendly smile accompanied by the words, "I hope Doha wasn't too much of a burden during the trip." Indicating the several small pieces of hand luggage I was carrying, I answered lightly, "Apart from these small burdens, not at all."

He chuckled as he reached out to take the luggage from me. "This is exactly what I mean. You must have wasted half your time in Rome helping her shop."

"Doha has much more experience at that and better taste than I do; she certainly didn't need my help."

I examined his face. His straight chestnut hair was combed back off his forehead and was as carefully styled and trimmed as his mustache. His wide hazel eyes seemed fixed in a startled stare and this, together with a mouth that seemed permanently poised to smile, gave him an almost infantile expression. In Rome, I occasionally imagined this moment with dread. I wondered how I would react when I met the man whom I had betrayed before ever setting eyes on him, the man whom I had intended to permanently deprive of Doha when I married her. As I observed him now, however, I did not feel guilty; nor could I bring myself to do so. I was too numb to feel anything at all.

Hatem, who was driving Samira and me home, asked me endless questions about Rome and my experiences there. The brevity of my answers prompted him to ask, more anxiously than before, "What's the matter with you? Why are you so thin and distracted? Most people come back from Europe happy, not half dead."

I forced myself to concentrate. "Don't worry, Hatem. It's just the flu and fatigue from the journey. A couple of home-cooked meals by Samira and I'll be back to normal."

As he dropped us off in front of our house, Hatem said, "Maybe you should rest at home two or three days before coming back to work."

"I'll see. Anyway, my job isn't very taxing, as you know."

Inside the house, Samira hugged me again and said, "I missed you. You don't know how much I missed you." She spoke rapidly, a bit nervously. She, too, was shocked by my appearance. She hugged me again, then stood back and contemplated me at arm's length. "But really, what is wrong with you? Hatem's right. You look half dead. Are you really just worn out from the trip?"

"Yes."

I stayed home the following day; Samira had insisted I keep her company. "I was almost climbing the walls all by myself in this big house. I was dying for someone to speak to," she said.

"Why didn't you try to do some reading, Samira? It would have at least kept you occupied. The house is full of books."

She pouted her lips and said, "Reading only makes me more bored." She looked around the room. "If only, instead of all these books, you'd . . . ." But she cut herself short.

After completing preparatory school at the French lycée, Samira—in deference to our father's wishes—remained housebound, as had her sister, Suad, before she married. She was as beautiful as Suad, in her own way, having inherited very few of our mother's features and resembling our father more closely than Suad or me. Her exposure to life outside the home was very limited: the only news and information she obtained was from her old school friends, and their number had gradually diminished as they married off one by one. One of her few sources of entertainment were those magazines that feature the latest gossip about film stars and other celebrities. These she bought regularly, in spite of her general aversion to reading.

Samira had a surprise in store for me that first day after my return, when I stayed home with her instead of reporting to work. She sprang it on me over lunch. "Listen," she said. "I've been thinking a lot while you were away and I've made a decision."

I was taken aback by her unaccustomed assertiveness. I'd always pampered her, unable to regard her as anything but my baby sister even though she was now twenty-four. I gestured for her to continue.

"Listen. I can't go on this way; it's been driving me crazy, especially after Suad and you left home. I want to work, and I want you to help me find a job."

I was at a loss for words. I had never so much as pictured Samira (or Suad for that matter) working for a living. In this respect I was like my father. I saw it as my duty to support my sisters until a suitable groom came along and then to provide their trousseau when he did. Also, I was afraid I would hurt Samira's feelings by telling her that she would never find a decent job with a preparatory school education as her only qualification. She must have read my thoughts because she said, "I know my degree isn't worth much. But I'm going to learn how to type on a foreign typewriter and I still remember most of my French. I'm willing to work anywhere. Please help." Her eyes brimmed with tears.

"I'll try, Samira. I don't know exactly what to do yet, but I'll figure something out." Her eyes continued to implore me, tears now overflowing the rims and trickling down her cheeks. "You can start your typing lessons tomorrow if you want," I said. "By the time you've finished, you'll have a job waiting for you."

I had no idea how I was going to make that happen, but I must have sounded confident enough. Her face lit up, and she came around to my side of the table and kissed me on the forehead.

The next day I went to work. The first familiar face I saw was Mustafa's. He bellowed a hearty greeting and emerged from his kiosk to shake my hand. "Welcome back! Europe, man! Some people have all the luck. What I wouldn't give for a few months at the top of the world!"

"But our country is beautiful, too, Mustafa. Don't you know that this is where civilization has its roots?"

He scanned the area around us, his eyes coming to rest without expression on the broadcasting building. "I didn't mean anything, sir," he mumbled, after which he raised his voice to proclaim, "Everybody knows that Egypt's the mother of the world and that its president is the bravest president in the world." He then glanced furtively over his shoulders to ascertain that no one was within hearing distance, leaned toward my ear while pretending to study the shop window in front of us, and lowered his voice again to say, "Did you bring any cigarettes or whiskey with you from abroad? There aren't that many customers anymore, but for you I'll do my best. Dollars are in high demand, too, these days, if you happen to have any left over."

"I'm not a trader, Mustafa."

He jerked back as though stung. "What shame is there in trade? It's a very noble profession, sir."

"Of course it is. I'm just not a trader, that's all."

He sighed and added in a low grumble, "As if there was any business left to trade in anyway. When, God willing, will things return to normal, like they were before?"

It was time to change the subject. "Have you seen Qinawi while I was away? Did he get another leave?"

Mustafa's eyes widened in surprise. "Leave? Haven't you heard?"

My heart leaped in alarm. "No. What happened?"

"The poor guy. He lost his leg in the war. He's in the hospital."

I went up to my office. It was empty. I rang Hatem. "That's right," he said. "I didn't want to tell you right away when you got back. Sayyid's in a rehabilitation center now."

14

S tepping off the tram at the stop near the rehabilitation center I encountered dozens of khaki-clad soldiers pushing wheelchairs in which sat men with only a single arm or a single leg protruding from their white hospital gowns, or, in some instances, no arms or legs at all. There was no need to ask directions; I simply fell in with the ragged train of soldier-driven wheelchairs, careful to avoid eye contact with their occupants. Occasionally, a wheelchair would park in front of one of the sidewalk fruit vendors whose oranges and tangerines were arranged in neat tiny pyramids that glistened alluringly in the sun. I paused to buy some oranges before reaching my destination.

Hatem had given me Sayyid's room number, but the room was empty. As I stepped back into the corridor I spotted a nurse pushing a wheelchair upon which sat a man whose face was entirely wrapped in gauze. She told me that none of the patients were in their rooms at present. They were all out by the swimming pool. I left the bag of oranges in Sayyid's room and went back downstairs in the direction she'd indicated.

The swimming pool, with its blue water, sparkled dazzlingly. The garden area around it was mostly populated by wheelchairs, but there was something almost festive about the white hospital gowns of their occupants, the khaki uniforms of their attendants, the brightly colored clothes of visitors, the shouts of children who had left their parents to play on the grass, the clatter of dice on backgammon boards, and the whoops of laughter. Sayyid spotted me first. He called out my name and I caught sight of him waving to me from the middle of the crowd and starting to roll his wheelchair in my direction. I rushed over to him to keep him from making the effort. When I drew up, he used one hand on the armrest to lift his torso upward and the other hand to clap my shoulder as I bent over to embrace him.

"When did you get back, sir?" he asked cheerfully.

"Two days ago. But I only found out about . . . . I only learned you were here, today."

I pulled over one of the bamboo chairs that were scattered around the garden and sat facing him. Forcing a smile, I said, "Welcome back to you. I suppose it could have been worse. Some fates are easier to bear than others, as we say in my village."

Sayyid rocked with laughter and waved his hand as though to contradict me. "You should be congratulating me, sir. They're going to pay me a huge compensation." He spread his hands apart to illustrate how huge. "It'll be enough to build a house for my children and to make the pilgrimage—they're going to give me precedence in the pilgrimage lottery. On top of that, they're going to fit me out with a leg that looks exactly like a real one." He patted the empty fabric of his hospital gown where his leg had once been and laughed. "In fact, the doctors say that it works better than a real leg."

I smiled feebly and said, "But all that doesn't make up for the sacrifice you made, Sayyid."

"What sacrifice, sir? You sound just like Mr. Hatem and the Moral Guidance people." Then he broke into a broad smile, leaned over and whispered, "By the way, Moral Guidance has really done a good job here. I've never seen people laugh as much as the patients do here. It's their visitors who are depressed. It shows on their faces."

The observation stunned me. I looked around and noticed that, indeed, most of the occupants of the wheelchairs were huddled over lively games of backgammon and engaged in animated banter. Their open, gleeful faces stood in glaring contrast to the frowns and averted eyes of their visitors. I leaned toward Sayyid and, lowering my voice to the requisite confidential pitch, I asked, "But how did Moral Guidance manage to get these results?"

"They talked an awful lot. But, I think that mostly it was because they just put us together and let us be. Forced to manage on our own, we all started to do as much as we could to help and comfort others until gradually we started to feel normal again. But tell me, sir, are you ill or something? Forgive me, but you've changed a lot. You're as thin as a rail."

I gave him the line about the flu. He shook his head and said anxiously, "You should take care, sir."

After a brief silence, I asked, "How did you get out of Yemen, Sayyid?"

"On my left leg." Greatly amused by his own joke, he amplified, "For the sake of Mina and for Gamal Abdel Nasser and for your sake, sir, I left my right leg behind in Yemen."

"It hurts me to hear you say that Sayyid. It makes me feel in some way responsible for the loss of your leg."

"That's not what I meant at all, sir. I was trying to reassure you that I've been learning on my own, like you once told me to do. Real life over there taught me a lot, and I began to understand many of the things I used to ask you about. When the imam's men attacked us at night, shooting at us from the tall houses in the mountains, we had some Yemeni farmers with us. Some of them didn't know how to fire a gun, but they'd fetch the ammunition and point out the houses where the spies and snipers were hiding—those houses belonged to some of the country's top officials." He leaned toward me and resumed in an even lower hush than before, "But, sir, our men . . . many of them fought like men, but there were some others —the kind who loaded airplanes with refrigerators, washing machines and foreign cigarettes to send back to Egypt—these ones, when they were put to the test. . . ."

He broke off, flopped back in his chair and ran his hand over his bristly scalp. "The farmers who were helping us were in as much danger as we were. Many of them were wounded. When the shrapnel tore into my leg, they were the ones who carried me to the medical unit. As for the imam's men, the first thing they did when they entered the village was to burn down the wooden schoolhouse I told you about, the one our engineers built out of ammunition crates."

"The imam's men know who their enemy is, Sayyid."

He turned and stared into a remote distance and said, "Maybe they do, but we don't." He brought his focus back to me and continued in a low voice, "You know those tall houses where the sniper fire came from, the ones where the spies and the imam's men hid out and which belonged to Yemen's bigwigs? Our own army commanders and government officials visited those houses, bringing expensive gifts and gold. With that gold, our enemies bought the weapons that killed us."

He looked away again and fell silent. Unconsciously, I followed his gaze. A physiotherapist in a swimming suit was standing at the edge of the pool, bellowing instructions to a man in the water in the loud rat-a-tat of an athletics coach. The man in the pool would sink underwater for a long time then resurface, coughing and sputtering, and reach for the edge of the pool. But the therapist would bend down and say, "Good! Good, Captain. But what did we say? No, that won't do. We're not going to get out now, not after all this progress. The next time you'll do even better. Come on, let's keep going. Now what did we say? The arm's supposed to do the work of the missing leg, and even more . . . ."

I doubted whether the man in the water heard any of this, what with all his coughing and wheezing. His arms thrashed the water as he groaned loudly and miserably as though calling out for help. Meanwhile, the therapist kept repeating, "As we said, the arm's supposed to do the work of the leg and more. Come on, keep going . . . ."

I turned my attention back to Sayyid. Two children were standing nearby. Not yet five, their hair was closely cropped with the exception of a long patch over their foreheads. They were wearing shirts and trousers made out of a cheap fabric and their deep black eyes were slightly sunken. There was no need for Sayyid to point to them and tell me that they were his sons, Salah and Khalid.

He beckoned them closer and said, "Come on, say hello to your uncle."

The children remained rooted where they stood, clinging to one another as they stared at me with a mixture of fear and shyness.

Sayyid looked at them and said, "Do you think they'll have it better than we do?"

But the question was not really directed at me, and he didn't expect an answer.

15

When Samira started her typing lessons her enthusiasm seemed boundless. Once she had a job, she said, she would go to night school and work toward a secondary school degree and then maybe go on to university. Hatem had told me that I would have little difficulty finding a job for Samira. It was now national policy to guarantee a job in the government bureaucracy to anyone with a preparatory school certificate or higher, and he advised me to submit her papers to the newly formed Ministry of Labor. I took his advice and then pulled whatever strings I could in order to ensure that she would be attached to a government department close to home. Samira would check the mailbox several times a day. When her official letter of appointment did arrive, she jumped up and down and squealed with joy, stopping to hug me every now and then and say, "How am I ever going to thank you? How am I ever going to thank you?"

It was around that time that Abd al-Magid entered my life. A graduate of the School of Commerce, he had been recently hired by the accounts department in the same ministry I worked in. He appeared in my office one day to introduce himself. He was tall and lanky and his thick, black hair glistened with grease. He told me that he was from the same village as my family and that we were distantly related on my father's side. He was proud to have made the acquaintance of such an important official as myself. He regarded me as the "dean of the family" and the "dean of the Qanatir area in Cairo." I took an instant dislike to him. But he kept dropping in.

Fortunately, I never stayed in the office long. Doha was rarely there as well. She had suddenly become very busy and would only pass by the office to collect some papers to take back to the ministry building where she would remain most of the day. But I was still determined to avoid encountering her, so after signing in I would leave again and while away the better part of the day in a coffeehouse. Yes, I had joined the thousands engaged in that habitual pastime of hanging out in sidewalk cafés and watching passersby—or, in my case, just staring out into space. The coffeehouse I settled upon was located in the Bab al-Luq district, within a five-minute walk from my office, and there I would stay until the time came to go back to the office and sign out, after which I would return to the coffeehouse. Gradually I developed a small group of acquaintances. Sometimes we would play backgammon, but mostly we talked away the hours. I discovered an amazing world that I had never known existed, a world of nothingness where Doha was as remote as could be, a specter that sometimes hovered at the edge of the grave.

Among my new coffeehouse friends was a man known only as "the Doctor." How he came by this name is a mystery. He was always elegantly turned out in a white silk shirt, gold wire-rimmed spectacles, and golden cufflinks sparkling at the ends of his sleeves. I was told that he had once been a medical school student, but was caught cheating on his exams and expelled. He introduced himself to me as a real estate agent. Others warned me that he was a pimp. I didn't care one way or the other. He was always up for a game of backgammon and he was an entertaining conversationalist, with a store of hundreds of anecdotes, mostly about women.

One evening I told the Doctor the following story: A friend of mine fell in love with a woman who was engaged to another man. The woman told him she loved him too, and even slept with him. She promised that she would break off her engagement. But suddenly she broke off the relationship and returned

108

to her fiancé. My friend, I told him, was going crazy because he could not understand why she had promised herself to him and why she then returned to her fiancé.

The Doctor paid close attention as I spoke. When I had finished, he smiled and said, as he combed his graying hair with his fingers, "I've heard many similar stories. Women are enigmas to those who don't know them and easy to read to those who do. Men fantasize about having sex with many women. They think that this is an exclusively male trait. But the fact is that women also fantasize about having sex with many men, and they would, too, if there weren't so many obstacles in their way."

"But what about love, Doctor?" I protested.

That elicited a derisive snicker. He put one hand in his trouser pocket, tapped it with the other and said, "Love is this," indicating his wallet. Then he pushed his pocketed hand toward his groin, tapped it again and said, "And this."

Exactly how a pimp would think, I thought to myself. I let my mind stray as he recounted a story about a woman he knew who left her husband after thirty years because he had lost both "this" and "this." Yet, I could not help wondering whether there was some truth to his words. Doha had known from the outset that I was far from rich. When we made love, she seemed contented. She even told me so. But was she telling the truth?

The Doctor snapped me out of my reverie with an invitation to a game of backgammon. Generally, the few piasters we would wager with would shift back and forth between us. But that night I experienced one of those rare occurrences that every player dreams of. I was on a roll. I'd call out the numbers before I rolled the dice, "Six, one," and I'd roll a six and a one; "Double five," and double five it would be. There was simply no way I could lose. My winning streak infuriated the Doctor and goaded him into demanding one set after the other. He grew more and more agitated with each successive game until, finally, he lost all the money he had on him.

"All right," he said, his eyes flashing with determination. "One more game for all the money you have on you."

"And what do I get if I win?" I taunted.

He narrowed his eyes and fixed them on me. "The most beautiful woman you've ever set eyes on."

"Let's play then."

The Doctor lost again. He slammed the backgammon board shut and said with barely suppressed anger, "Let's go. But you pay the taxi. And give the woman a tip."

We drove toward the Citadel. After we passed that the Doctor began to guide the taxi driver through a maze of narrow, unpaved roads with silent tombs on either side. We were in the City of the Dead, Cairo's oldest cemetery.

I laughed and whispered, "Did you bring me here to get laid or to bury me?"

"It all amounts to the same thing."

The taxi thumped onto a paved road again and began to wend between small, crudely built two- or three-story buildings. At a small roundabout, we left the taxi waiting and continued on foot through a series of narrow alleys. We turned into one of those buildings and climbed up to the second floor, where the Doctor rapped a private signal on a pane of glass set into the apartment door. A woman appeared. She was every bit as beautiful as he had claimed—both her face and her body—although when she opened the door she had her hair wrapped in a kerchief, a sheen of perspiration covered her forehead, and her oval face was still slightly flushed from sleep. In a weary voice, she invited us in and ushered us into a sitting room. In it was a rustic couch—a wooden frame topped by an upholstered mattress, a couple of upholstered cushions propped against the wall and a couple of bolsters in the same fabric to serve as armrests—and two worn chairs placed facing one another at right angles to the couch. As I took a seat my nose was assaulted by the unmistakable odor of salt-cured mullet. She and the Doctor had disappeared into another room from which I could hear her say in a plaintive voice, "I told you not to bring them so late, Doctor, so that I can be ready to receive them. I said before dinner, not in the middle of the night. Now my face is all puffed up with sleep. Is that what you want?" And I overheard the Doctor say, "Shut up woman. You're a jinx. I lost you in a game of backgammon so I won't be making a tin piaster out of you tonight. Now get it over with. I'll be waiting in the taxi in the square." Then I heard him leave and the door click shut behind him. A short while later the woman came back into the sitting room. She had washed her face and removed the kerchief to allow her long, silky chestnut hair to tumble over her naked white shoulders and over her prominent bosom. She had changed into a red rayon shift that ended several inches above her knees, and she had applied lipstick, but so hastily that she missed the corners of her mouth and created a lopsided circle beneath her finely chiseled nose. She sat down on the couch next to me, with the two bolsters separating us, and brought one foot up beneath the thigh of the other leg.

"Welcome, welcome. Can I get you dinner?"

"No, thank you."

"So you've eaten?"

She inclined toward me as she said that, causing the shoulder strap of her dress to slip down and bringing the luminous skin of her softly curving shoulder beneath my nose. I edged closer. She took hold of my hand and lowered her eyes seductively. "Are you sure you've eaten? Or is it me you want to eat?" At this point an audible yawn escaped her and I was overwhelmed by the smell of the musky breath of sleep mixed with the penetrating odor of salt-cured mullet tinged with mint. I put my hand in my pocket to take out some money for a "tip" so that I could leave and join the Doctor in the taxi, but she placed her hand over her mouth and said in a child-like whimper, "Shame on me. Please forgive me. I was sleepy. I'm sorry." I placed my hand on her velvety shoulder and I bent over to kiss her. "It's okay, it's okay, it's okay. . . ." I mumbled as I continued to kiss her mouth and her mullet and her mint.

"Right here?"

I removed the bolsters. "Yes, here."

She was breathing heavily and between intermittent giggles she said, "Damn you, did you have to come for a late-night snack? Why didn't you come for dinner?"

I doubled the amount of money I was going to give her.

At the time, it seemed like life would simply go on this way. I regained all the weight I had lost and considerably more. The fever had broken and all that remained were a few blisters, invisible to everyone but myself.

The music had faded and my life settled into a protracted silent whine that I found almost soothing and even enjoyable. Its rhythm was marked by the rattling of the dice and the clatter of the backgammon pieces, the clinking of glasses and dishes, the creaks of doors opening and closing, water whooshing from faucets, thumps on the back in greeting, barks of laughter, and the hush of whispers. I was in a continuous semi-coma floating between a kind of wakefulness during the day and oblivion at night. Occasionally, out of this torpor there would sound the old processional drumbeat—or rather an echo of the old drumbeat, but sudden and powerful—and Doha would resurface from between the lines of something I was reading or through the miasma of the perfume of a hired woman in my arms and catch me off guard. Then the echo would fade as suddenly as it had begun, and life would resume its familiar stillness.

Even Samira's wedding came and went without ruffling my newly found equanimity, although it would have a profound impact on my life. Presenting his request for my sister's hand, my ministry colleague and distant cousin Abd al-Magid told me that he felt it would be a great honor to become the brother-in-law of the family dean in Cairo. I almost turned him down out of hand. But, on second thought, I felt that my sister should have the right to decide. I raised the matter with Samira with little enthusiasm and she asked to meet him. Afterward she said that she had no objection to marrying him. Abd al-Magid did all that was required of him. He produced the necessary engagement jewelry and the dowry, and I put all the money I had saved from my study grant into purchasing new furniture for Samira. Abd al-Magid specified his wishes in this regard item by item, after which he kept close track of the manufacture of every piece. Soon I discovered that my savings would not stretch far enough, so I took out a loan against my salary. Then, after all the furniture was completed and the marriage contract signed, Samira informed me that Abd al-Magid had been unable to find an apartment and that he asked permission to live with us after the wedding ceremony "until circumstances improved." For Samira's sake I had to agree. We piled up most of our old furniture in a spare room and crammed the remainder into my bedroom. They had the house to themselves most of the time since I had taken up permanent residence in the coffeehouse with the Doctor and our backgammon games.

So why, after surrendering my body and soul to dissipation, did I erupt into that rage? Why did I pound my fists on Hatem's desk one day and bellow unintelligible howls because words wouldn't form themselves, until finally I managed to roar, "Why did you do that?" I only snapped out of it at the sight of Hatem's pleading eyes and the sound of his low, desperate voice imploring, "Please, I beg you. Not here. Not in the office. You'll ruin me." I stood paralyzed and mute until, somehow, I managed to find the door and stumble out of his office.

I trod the streets for hours. I must have been talking to myself out loud, judging by the alarmed stares I received—not that I cared. Maybe Hatem was telling the truth, I thought. Maybe my eyes deceived me. Maybe he really was just whispering something in Doha's ears. . . . No! When I opened the door to his office he was kissing her on her cheek, wasn't he? Then, when he caught sight of me he only pretended to be whispering something in her ear. So he kissed her. What business is it of mine? It's over between us. Can't you get that through your head? The old ghost arose. So what? Put it to rest. You're a backgammon player now. You're one of the Doctor's friends and you visit the women in the City of the Dead. You tried to learn the names of flowers once, but now you've forgotten them, and your pockets are empty. But there's still Aset in Thebes, isn't there? In the chamber to your right after you enter the temple. Aset, who married her brother Osiris and gave birth to a hawk . . . who sometimes wears a gown made of feathers . . . whose hair is black and whose eyes are rimmed with kohl . . . who crosses the heavens in the sky-bark with her father Ra. Would she help me if I went there? Went where? What was I trying to say?

Eventually, my feet took me back to apartment block where my office was located. I went upstairs and opened the door. She was sitting behind her desk. What did she see in my face? She rose to her feet. With her upper body crouched forward, supported by her hands on her desk, she seemed ready to pounce. She pinned me with the glare of a predatory bird and lashed out in an even hiss, "Not one word."

"I'll show you," I said with a demented laugh and walked out.

Shukri sounded alarmed when I called him. "Has something happened to Doha?"

"No. No need to worry. Aset's fine."

"Who?"

"You can call her yourself, if you want to put your mind to rest. I called you about something else. Yes, it's quite urgent. Can we meet in Lappas?" I asked, naming the first European-style café that sprang to mind.

After a moment's silence Shukri said, "Please tell Doha what this urgent matter is, and she can tell me later."

"Listen," I said with growing impatience, "I want to talk to you about something that happened in Rome, something that concerns you."

He fell silent again and then said, "Please have Madam Doha inform me what you have to say."

I said good-bye and hung up.

The following day I went to the office, late as usual, and found Doha there again. All her desk drawers were open and she was handing files and assorted papers to the office boy standing next to her.

"Good morning," I said.

She returned the greeting nonchalantly, without looking at me. But then she said, "I hope the person who comes to replace me will be better than me."

"Why? Where are you going?"

"I've been transferred," she said in the same offhand tone.

She handed a piece of paper to me. I unfolded it. It was a printed ministerial decree. Following the customary preamble containing her name in full, it stated, "Firstly, the aforementioned has been promoted to Director of the Office of the First Deputy Minister of the Ministry of . . . ."

Doha remained behind after the office boy left. She stared at me coldly for a moment, then said, "What the hell were you trying to do? When will it sink in that it's over between us? For good!"

She swiveled toward the door and strode out of the room. She was through with that office, and with me, forever.

16

Meanwhile, there were developments on the home front. Samira soon began to share her husband's enthusiasm for socialism and the Socialist Union Party. She joined the party's so-called 'Committee of Twenty' in the government department where she worked and her conversations in the house were now heavily peppered with such expressions as "bureaucratic elevation," "point of order," and "retrograde elements." Also, within a few months after marrying Samira and moving in, Abd al-Magid stopped hailing me as "dean of the family and the village" and began to peg me as "retrograde element." He initially he tossed the label at me as a witty taunt, but eventually it became a permanent epithet that he felt entitled to bestow on me in his capacity as a committed socialist.

This was not long after Sayyid al-Qinawi, having been equipped with an artificial limb and released from hospital, had resumed his old job at the ministry. The ministry was holding new elections and he wanted me to join his list. "Fine. Feel free to add my name, if you want to guarantee that your list loses," I jested. But when he began to turn up every day in my office to press me, I resolved to put a stop to it. "Listen, Sayyid," I said firmly, "I don't want to have anything to do with that business. Put Hatem's name on the list."

"His name's already at the top of the list," he countered. "When I told Mr. Hatem that I wanted to nominate you, he said that it was his greatest wish that you'd join us."

That took me aback. I had barely seen Hatem since the day I caught him kissing Doha, and on the few occasions that I did see him, neither of us broached that subject. If we happened to bump into one another in the ministry's corridors, we greeted each other jovially as though the incident had never occurred and we were the same old buddies we had always been.

Sayyid's dark eyes regarded me from their deep recesses. "So tell me, why don't you want to nominate yourself?" he asked. "If it's the wrong thing to do, I won't nominate myself either. I just wish you'd explain."

"Sayyid, these are the elections to the leadership board. That means that anyone who nominates themselves wants to lead people. Anyone who wants to lead has to know what they're about. So, if I, personally, don't know what I'm about, how can I possibly lead others?"

"So I know what I'm about?" he asked satirically.

"Yes, Sayyid, you do," I answered seriously. "And Hatem does too. But me, I'm one of those 'retrograde elements,' as my brother-in-law Abd al-Magid calls me."

Sayyid's face soured at the mention of that name. He said, "Did you know that he nominated himself on the First Deputy Minister's list?"

"So I heard."

"Sultan Bek is the root of corruption in the ministry. Every piece of swindling and skullduggery passes across his desk. Did you know that he has the ministry's workers building a villa for him and that he's paying them out of the ministry budget? Did you know. . . ."

I cut him off impatiently. "No I didn't know and I don't want to know. It's got nothing to do with me."

Sayyid stood to leave. In a voice thick with dismay he said, "I'd really hoped I could persuade you, sir. You'd have been a great asset to us."

"And who's this 'us' exactly?" I asked, as I rose to see him off.

"The list . . . of candidates who stand against corruption."

I laughed and said, "You give me way too much credit. Still, I hope you win."

In fact, Sayyid, Hatem, and six or seven others from their list did win. Nevertheless, the majority of the victors were from the First Deputy Minister's list, and one of these was Abd al-Magid.

Life at home was growing tenser by the day. Abd al-Magid had Samira account for every last piaster she spent on the meals she prepared. After dinner, he'd take up pen and paper and calculate the household expenses, itemizing every piece of fruit he had bought the day before and the lemons he bought after Friday prayers, and then divide the sum by three. When, after that painstaking adding, multiplying and dividing, he'd offer to show me the results, I would wave his calculations away and tell him that I trusted him. Then, on the first of the month, he'd bring out his bundle of papers and tell me I owed him so and so many pounds, which I would hand over to him without further discussion. Eventually, to rid my mouth of that sour taste, I announced one day that I would not eat at home anymore. He eyed me scornfully and said, "Fine. Go spend your money on restaurants instead of on your sister. Be your usual retrograde self." I refused to rise to the bait. For Samira's sake I always took pains to avoid an argument with him. So ardently did she dote on him that she regarded him as a model of rectitude and deferred to his every decision. From that day onward I only returned home in order to sleep.

In the coffeehouse, where I spent the greater part of the day, I switched from backgammon to chess, after discovering that it was an excellent way to pass the time and barely gave me a chance to think of food. My companions and I would wolf down sandwiches and sip at a succession of teas and coffees as we contemplated the playing boards in silence, whether we were playing ourselves, or observing the moves of other contestants. Before you knew it, a good ten hours had elapsed. At night, in bed, I'd kick myself for having overlooked a perfect move I could have made with the knight or I'd smile smugly at the naiveté of a player who had fallen so easily in the trap I'd laid for him by sacrificing a pawn. Eventually, I'd lull myself to sleep concocting new opening gambits for the next day's sessions. My mind had become a field of black and white squares upon which roamed queens, bishops, and rooks.

From time to time, Sayyid would drop by the office to say goodbye before heading off to some European or Asian country in the company of an Egyptian socialist delegation. Whenever he asked me whether I needed anything from abroad, I'd tell him to bring me a book on chess—about the only type of book I touched nowadays. He would also drop by regularly to complain about First Deputy Sultan Bek and the band of thieves who operated under his protection. Generally, I'd just sit and listen, but on one occasion I said, "You seem to have become quite an important man in the Socialist Union, judging by all those trips you make abroad. Instead of telling me about Sultan Bek's dirty dealings, why don't you report them to the people in the Socialist Union so they can take action against him?"

He reacted as though I had just cracked a splendid joke. When he recovered from laughing he said, "That's because he's much higher up than I am in the Union. Sultan Bek's way up there, at the top." He swung his arm toward the ceiling to point to that lofty height.

Even so, I sensed that Sayyid al-Qinawi was much more important than he let on. Rumors were circulating about an underground organization within the Socialist Union and I was sure that he was a member. Not that I asked him to confirm this or that he ever volunteered the information.

Although I hadn't shown the slightest interest in the corruption in the ministry and the part the First Deputy played in it, Sayyid appointed me his advisor on the problems in the leadership committee. He began to complain to me about people on his list. They—"even Hatem"—had begun to toady up to Sultan Bek and turn a blind eye to the corruption.

He confided such grievances in a near whisper, although there was no one around to hear us. I had the office pretty much to myself now that Doha had been transferred. No replacement had been sent, so the Supervisory Board for Administrative Organization had shrunk even further to those two or three temporary exiles who had incurred the wrath of their superiors and who came and went as they pleased. As the most senior staff member, I was now the de facto head of my department.

On one occasion, Sayyid walked in, at about one o'clock as usual, looking despondent. He took a seat in front of my desk and remained mute. "What's the matter this time? Has Sultan Bek been up to his usual tricks?"

He seemed nervous and preoccupied as he answered. "Yes, I've discovered something very important, but I had to wait until I could get hold of the proof." Suddenly he burst out, "They want to ruin me, sir!" He glanced quickly at the doorway and lowered his voice. "I met Mr. Hatem today. He told me to watch out because they're putting a rumor around the Ministry that I'm a leftist."

I gave a dismissive shrug and said, "You're the one who chose to go down that path. It's no good complaining about it now."

This puzzled him. "But doesn't the president say in every speech that we have to fight corruption? Doesn't he say that this is our country and that if we let the big shots ruin it, it will come crashing down on our heads? I know everything: what Sultan Bek gets up to, the bribes the lady who used to sit in that desk over there gets, and the cut she takes before handing the rest to Sultan Bek. I know about the forged checks and the fake conference per diems. So why is it that when I speak about those things they treat me like I'm the guilty one and call me a leftist?" He frowned and paused as though struck by something. "By the way," he resumed, "I swear that I don't even know what that word means! I've heard it in the president's speeches and sometimes they fling it around in the leadership committee. But I have no idea what 'leftist' means exactly. Is it something very bad?"

I thought for a moment and then said, "Everywhere else in the world it means one thing; here it means another. Here 'leftist' is about the same as 'communist.'"

"Oh my God!" he moaned as the blood drained from his face.

"That's why Hatem was right to caution you," I said.

"I swear, sir, that when we went to East Germany, I never left the Deputy Minister's side. I don't know any foreign languages and I never spoke to a soul."

I sighed. "You don't have to defend yourself to me. I haven't accused you of anything. I only wanted to caution you, like Hatem did. You're not as strong as Sultan Bek. You yourself told me that he is a powerful man, even in the Socialist Union."

He stared morosely at his feet. He hadn't been listening to me; his mind was elsewhere. Eventually, he said dejectedly, "That's what they used to do in Yemen. The imam's people would tell the farmers not to pray in the same mosque as the Egyptians. Egyptians are heretics, they said. They're socialists and socialists are heretics. Many Yemenis believed this and left the mosque to us." He seemed to have been speaking into a void when he said that, but suddenly he turned to me, his eyes burning with resentment. "But to hell with their accusations!" he said in a low growl. "I saw death with my own eyes in Yemen, and I prayed for the dead. I saw my leg fly off. It could have been my head. For weeks I was between life and death. I'm not going to become a coward now just because they . . . ."

The rest was choked off. He stood abruptly and rushed to the door. But suddenly he stopped and turned back. "Anyway, that's not why I came to see you. I had something important to tell you. I almost forgot. I was going to tell Mr. Hatem myself, but I couldn't bring myself to do it. You're his lifelong friend, so I think it would be better if it came from you."

121

He seemed sad, almost apologetic. I looked at him in anticipation of the rest. After a moment's silence, he resumed uncomfortably, "Tell Mr. Hatem to stop going to Madam Doha's house to play poker. The police know that she's running a gambling den, and they have her house under surveillance."

Sayyid left the room so quickly that he didn't hear my question, "How did you find out about that, Sayyid?"

Maybe I hadn't even uttered the question out loud.

17

This was hardly the first time that Sayyid brought the subject of you up, Doha, having decided to keep me abreast of your activities in your new office next to Sultan Bek. I would listen to his stories with feigned indifference and, perhaps, no small amount of malice. I'd think, Ha! Look how low she's fallen. She was far from the person I had made her out to be. She was never Aset. I'd fallen in love with her and like all lovers I had placed her on a pedestal. I had imagined her high-minded, ennobled by lofty ideas and poetry, exuding a fragrance of flowers and mystery, whereas, in fact, she was probably worse than other women—or so I kept telling myself. I believe I convinced myself that my feelings for you had died, Doha. "My feelings for her have died," I would repeat over and over again. Whole days would go by without some corner of my brain whispering your name or your face appearing to my mind's eye.

What exactly is this illness—this affliction that cannot be cured by any amount of oblivion, rounds of chess, hours of blindly roaming the streets, other women, conversations with the Doctor, Hatem, and Sayyid about sex, politics, corruption, the past, and the future? Why does that sailing wing fade to a distant point in the sky and vanish, only to suddenly swoop down again over my head, casting a vast shadow that obliterates all light and all sound, before it folds me into the clutch of its soft, predatory feathers and transports me far away from all sound and silence to a place remote from mankind where all that exists is love and despair, the font of life and the font of death,

123

and your face alone? What was I thinking that day when I raced up the stairs to your new office? Was it you I hoped to save? Or was I trying to save myself?

It was another Doha I saw there. She was still beautiful, but this Doha had thickly painted lips, enameled fingernails, and thinly plucked eyebrows that arched over cruel eyes. Her hands, with their long, lacquer-tipped fingers spread open, rested on an enormous desk. Behind her was a vinyl upholstered door with a red light bulb above it. Several employees stood in front of her desk, tentatively extending documents toward her, their bodies bent forward in servility, as stiff as wood. They addressed you as "Effendim" in tones that made this title of respect sound like "master." Your dark eyes regarded them coolly, commandingly, in full control. But when they fell on me they clouded with suspicion and your face hardened. You feared a scandal or some sort of danger. You asked me what you could do for me. You addressed me as "Effendim," but that was to demarcate a boundary.

I stammered out, "I need to speak to you about something important."

That this was the first time I had ever come to your office heightened your sense of foreboding. With a casual flick of the wrist you dismissed the underlings and instructed them to come back later. After they had left, you fixed me with a glassy stare, folded your hands upon your desk, and repeated, "Effendim?"

The fear beneath your iciness was almost palpable. I almost smiled. I felt like saying, "Don't put yourself to the trouble, Doha. You can't insult me more than you already have." I wanted to say, "Doha, even when you give me that stony glare as you sit there with your lacquered nails and plucked eyebrows in front of a vinyl upholstered door that hides a thief whom you've made your partner, I love you. When I look at you, I don't see your lipstick coated lips, your stiffly coiffed hairdo, and your predatory talons. You always appear to me in the midst of a rainy mist.

124

I see droplets like morning dew on your rounded cheeks, I smell fresh rain in your hair, and your voice sets sail to my longing for the chants of priestesses in the temple and the songs of mermaids in the sea. I love you so much! Be whomever you want. I will always see you through the prism of a rainy mist—even when you ask me, for the third time and with growing impatience, 'Effendim?'"

I could not force my voice to function. The words refused to come out as you sat there, watching me with barely suppressed anger and barely suppressed fear. I snatched a piece of paper from your desk and wrote on it with a trembling hand, "I've heard that the police are watching your house. You have to stop gambling." I held the paper up before your face and watched you read it uncomprehendingly, at first, and then read it again. Your eyes widened in alarm and your face blanched. You reached out to grab the paper, but I stuffed it into my pocket and left.

I found myself walking up flights of stairs and passing through a maze of corridors. I realized my feet were taking me to Hatem's office to caution him. Suddenly I stopped and told myself that it wasn't necessary now that I had warned Doha.

As I wandered those intersecting corridors with their high ceilings and rows of tall, grimy windows, I muttered, "Now, Doha, I've paid in full, haven't I? I've betrayed trust, I've betrayed justice, and I've betrayed myself. You couldn't ask for more, could you? What further tribute could I lay at your feet, Aset?"

18

As it turned out, it was Hatem who came to me. I was sitting at my desk the following morning reading who-knows-what when I glanced up and saw him standing in the doorway. For a frozen moment we stared at each other in silence. Finally, he closed the door and walked toward me. I stood to greet him, keeping the desk between us as a barrier as I stiffly reached my hand out to shake his. A look of deep sadness came into his face. He walked around to my side of the desk and pulled me into a strong hug. Then he stepped back, retaining a grip on my upper arms, and said, "Don't you know me? I'm Hatem. I'm your friend." There were tears in his eyes.

My voice quivered as I said, "Please, Hatem, sit down. We . . . we've never had to speak this way before."

"You're right," he said softly as he took a seat. "I've been waiting a long time for you to come and have it out with me, so we can put this problem behind us. I've also wanted to come to you to settle it, but I was too ashamed. I felt I'd betrayed you somehow."

Still rather nervous, I said, "Please, Hatem, let's not talk about this."

"But I want you to know the truth."

"I don't want to hear it."

He shook his head and remained silent for a moment. Then he said, "Sayyid al-Qinawi came to me today. He thought you'd already spoken to me about a certain matter."

"So you got the message?"

"Yes, but I wish it had come from you." He rubbed his hand through his hair, which had begun to gray at the temples. "Anyway, that's all over. The fever's gone."

I broke out into a long, hysterical laugh that made Hatem eye me curiously. "What's gotten into you?"

Between heaves of laughter, I managed to say, "So you hope, Hatem. So you hope. But that kind of fever doesn't go away so easily. Believe me."

"It seems like we're talking about two different things." He slapped the desk impatiently. "Or maybe we are talking about the same thing, but not in the way you think. That fever I was talking about. . . . No, forget that. Do you know who invited me to her house the first time? It was Shukri—that night when I first met him, while we were waiting for you at the airport. I took him up on his invitation. I had a good time, playing poker and chatting with him about this and that. But that isn't why I went. I couldn't admit to myself that it was her I came to see, that the only reason I went was to be near her. I didn't know what to expect. I tried, you know, but she turned me down. Well, she didn't exactly turn me down. She kept me dangling. That day in the office—yes, I was coming onto her, but she turned me down again. At her house, other people began to join in the game. Whether it was Shukri or Doha who invited them, I'm not sure. But as the circle of players grew, I saw myself falling further and further. Every evening, I'd head over there, feeling disgusted with myself. I'd tell myself, this is the last time. I'm never coming here again. Then, come the next night, at the very same time, wherever I happened to be—at home with the children, in the office, at the club, in a coffeehouse—I'd see her face and hear her whispering to me, and the next thing I knew I'd be there, sitting around the table playing cards with the others. But when I looked at the cards in my hand, it wasn't numbers, jacks, and kings that stared out at me, but her face. And instead of Shukri and all the other people who came every day, I saw only her, no one but her, though I knew perfectly well that I didn't stand a chance with her in the world. Even so . . . ."

"Even so, you'll keep going, Hatem," I interjected calmly, sympathetically.

"No," he said, halting the thought with his hand. "Believe me, all that's over. When Sayyid came to me today, I listened to him without uttering a word. I had to fight back my tears in front of him. I wasn't afraid of a scandal or anything like that. I thought of you and I thought of the old dreams we had together, and I pictured it all going down the drain at the gambling table. That's when something inside me told me I'd never go back there again."

In the same comforting tone I said, "I truly hope so, Hatem. But let's wait and see."

He looked shocked. "You don't believe me?"

"I believe you completely. I believe every word you've said. But that's not the point. Let's just wait and see."

"Please, don't try to make me doubt myself again," he said somewhat indignantly as he stood to leave. "I came to apologize, and now I'm asking you to help me."

I, too, stood and walked around the desk to him. "I betrayed you, once. Don't ask me how. But, please forgive me." I embraced him just as he had embraced me earlier, and my eyes moistened just as his had. But deep down I knew it was all hopeless. I knew that we were both, now, small, insignificant creatures trapped in the folds of those wings.

Not long after Hatem left, Sayyid al-Qinawi dropped by at his usual time. Contrary to his recent moroseness, he was grinning jubilantly as he limped energetically toward me. He leaned across my desk and confided gleefully, "Your friend, Sultan Bek, has fallen. And so has your friend, Madam Doha."

He settled himself on the chair that Hatem had just vacated and began to recount. As he had told me before, he had long known every detail of Doha's corrupt dealings: the amounts of money she exacted to pass documents into the first deputy's office, the price that had to be paid for Sultan Bek's signature, the type of gifts required in order to be nominated to committees that paid stipends, the bribes it took to secure an appointment on a delegation at home or abroad, the cuts Sultan Bek received from the construction contractors engaged to perform fictitious repairs to the ministry building, how exactly tenders came out in favor of this contractor or that, the buildings that were constructed at incredibly inflated costs and into whose pocket the difference went, and so on. But in spite of all this knowledge, he had still lacked the proof. Sultan Bek was an expert at playing his cards. He was almost impossible to beat. He had Doha as his screen, executing his orders. He was a powerful man in the ministry. He had several top officials, in fact the whole leadership board, in his pocket, and he obviously had some powerful backing from outside the ministry, although no one knew who this backing was and what form it took. When Sayyid presented this information to the Administrative Regulatory Board they told him, "We know all that, Sayyid, and much more. But where's the proof?" It was they who told him about the gambling den at Doha's house. They said, "We're keeping an eye on Sultan Bek and Doha, but, again, where's the proof?" Now, Sayyid said, he had the proof.

Throughout this whispered narrative Sayyid was constantly shooting wary glances toward the door. Now, he stood, limped quickly over to the door and locked it. I laughed. "Sayyid, there's nobody around. I'm the director here, and the secretary and coffee boy. Even the janitor hardly ever shows up."

"Even so," he said as he sat down again. He reached into his jacket pocket, pulled out a bundle of official forms and receipts, and thrust them toward me. "Take a look," he said triumphantly.

I looked but failed to follow. I recognized Doha's handwriting, of course. Scanning through some of the pages I read such entries as, "Bus rental," "Refreshments," "Lunch," "Reception,"

"Hotel accommodation," "Dinner," and so on. Next to each entry was a figure in Egyptian pounds.

"What's all this, Sayyid?" I asked.

"That's the trip the ministry's workmen took to Port Said," he answered with a chuckle. "It cost a whopping five thousand pounds. See, here's the total and here's the payment voucher from the accounts department. Madam Doha was the supervisor of that trip."

"So? Don't the workers have a right to take trips? In fact, there's an allocation for that in the ministry's budget."

"Yes, they have that right and, yes, there's an allocation. The only problem is that the trip never took place. No one went to Port Said. I asked each and every one of those men who are listed right here. Not a single one of them set foot in Port Said."

"How come?" I asked.

"How come?" he parroted as he slipped the papers back into his pocket. "I guess the regulatory board and the prosecutor's office will have an answer to that question."

"But, Sayyid, how did you get hold of those papers?"

"There are some decent people in every department of the ministry, sir. In fact, they're all decent, except for Sultan Bek and Doha and the likes of them."

"But that doesn't tell me how you got hold of those papers. That's spying, Sayyid."

He sprang to his feet and shot out, "We're talking about a gang of thieves, sir." He pounded his fist to his chest, saying, "This is my right and the right of all those workers whose signatures were forged on this list. Am I right or not?"

I refused to reply even as his eyes challenged me. After a moment of fighting to gain control over his voice he said, "Anyway, the regulatory board and the public prosecutor will look into the matter and the truth will come out. I'm going to hand the papers over to them and they'll do the rest." Then he leaned across my desk and added, "But I have a favor to ask. Don't breathe a word of this to anyone, not even to Mr. Hatem."

"All right," I answered, turning away uncomfortably.

But he remained stooped over my desk. For the first time since I'd known him he eyed me with suspicion. He smiled apologetically and said, "Swear to it."

I stared at him in shock. He held me in his gaze, that apologetic yet adamant smile still on his face. "Forgive me, sir. You've seen for yourself what they do. They call me a leftist."

I smiled back. But I took the oath.

Several days later, there were further developments at home. I had been avoiding Abd al-Magid as much as possible. Ever since he had made the acquaintance of the First Deputy Minister and was appointed to numerous stipend-paying committees, he would open his conversation with such remarks as, "When I met with His Excellency the Deputy, today . . ." or "As Sultan Bek told me in his office . . . ." Also, now that Samira was pregnant he had begun to act as though this added to his domestic stock. He would lie in wait for me until I came home at night in order to lecture me about my domestic duties and about the type of people who scrimped on their household expenses while squandering away their money in cafés and restaurants. But in addition to that, a new note had recently crept into his repertoire. He would now drop frequent insinuations about leftist elements and allusions to my friendship with Sayyid al-Qinawi. He must have said something to Samira, because at such points in his lectures she would grimace and turn away in disgust. Once, during a talk of this sort over breakfast, she couldn't restrain herself. "The left is going to destroy the Socialist Union and ruin the country!" she exclaimed.

Her outburst took me aback somewhat, but I countered, "And what exactly is 'the left,' Samira?"

"It's the ones who are insolent toward their superiors. We've got their sort in our department too. The left is . . . ." She turned to Abd al-Magid for help.

"Retrograde elements," he said with smug terseness.

"Yes, retrograde elements," she repeated, treating me to an accusing glare.

But Abd al-Magid had also become increasingly tense after Sayyid submitted his papers to the regulatory board, setting investigative procedures into motion. At the ministry, Sultan Bek's aides were going from office to office, putting it around that al-Qinawi had been recruited by retrograde elements to spread chaos in the ministry and that it was he who was currently under investigation in the Socialist Union because of this, as opposed to Sultan Bek who was a hundred percent clean. Naturally, Abd al-Magid was an energetic campaigner. At home, meanwhile, his remarks betrayed his growing anxiety. He grumbled that I put him in danger. Since everyone at the ministry knew that he was my brother-in-law, my connection with Sayyid al-Qinawi jeopardized his political future.

"To hell sixty times over with your political future!" I erupted on one of these occasions. "In fact, if your political future is ruined our country will have a better future."

He turned a pained expression to Samira. "You see?"

She looked at me sharply and intoned, "May God protect him and his future from evil."

While investigations were taking their course, Sultan Bek summoned me to his office. When I arrived, Doha signaled me to take a seat and engrossed herself in the papers on her desk. I, too, determinedly ignored her, focusing my attention on the window. Outside I saw the white apartment block in which my office was located and just beyond that the Stock Exchange building, its wooden windows half shut like drooping eyelids.

Finally, a bell went off on Doha's desk. Once again she signaled me, this time toward the vinyl upholstered door, and said, "Please, go in."

Sultan Bek's office was vast; it took me ages to cross the room. Heavy curtains hung over the windows and an air conditioner vibrated with a low, monotonous hum. Although there was a huge chandelier suspended over his head, it was turned off and, instead, several small lamps lit his desk. He remained silent, studying some papers in his hand as I walked toward him. Nor did he look up, greet me, or invite me to sit when I reached his desk. I settled myself into one of the massive upholstered armchairs in front of it.

Sultan Bek had a red, puffy face, his white hair was carefully slicked back, and every once in a while he'd raise his hand slowly and elegantly to adjust the gold-rimmed spectacles on the tip of his nose. I suddenly recalled a protest slogan we used to chant as students. It targeted Hafez Afifi and, through him, King Farouk: "Down with the Chief of the Royal Cabinet before the country goes down the toilet!" I smiled to myself. I don't know why that chant had sprung to mind. Sultan Bek bore absolutely no resemblance to Hafez Afifi.

Finally, Sultan Bek peered at me from across his desk. "And you would be . . . ." He read my name off a piece of paper on his desk. I acknowledged that the identification was correct. He resumed slowly, languidly, "The department you've been working in for years—that Supervisory Board for Administrative Organization—doesn't have much to keep it busy. The government's policy now is to increase production. I'm thinking of abolishing it."

"That's up to Your Excellency and the ministry."

Taking up the piece of paper containing my name, he swiveled in his chair to give me his profile. He moved the paper slightly away from his face as he said with indifference, "I see you know some foreign languages." When I failed to meet his expectation of a reply, he resumed in the same lackadaisical tone while continuing to peer at the paper as though on the verge of a decision, "If you do know foreign languages well, we could get you appointed to one of the ministry's bureaus abroad, in Europe or, perhaps, America. We need people there who know the languages."

"I hope I meet your expectations," I said.

He set down the paper, swiveled back to face me, and looked me in the face for the first time. "But working in the ministry's bureaus abroad is a very sensitive posting, as you know. Candidates must undergo intensive background investigations. So do you have any particular leanings?"

"No sir, I have no particular leanings."

He reclined in his chair and said, "That's odd. I heard you had a connection with certain elements in the leadership committee." He waved his hand in front of his face as though that were a minor concern. "Those retrograde elements are going to be crushed as a matter of course. The government is shifting to production and the revolution can have no mercy with the types who obstruct production. Our revolution has ways of dealing with saboteurs."

I remained silent.

He sighed and said, "You may leave now."

I started to leave, but he called me back after I had taken a few steps. Looking down at his papers again, he said, "I'll think about nominating you to a posting abroad. But you'd better sever your relations with all destructive elements. If you do, you'll be doing both them and yourself a favor. Goodbye."

I couldn't resist saying in the same calm tone, "Don't count on me on that score, Afifi Bek . . . excuse me, Sultan Bek."

But he simply waved me away and repeated, "Goodbye."

Outside the office, I said, "Tell that . . . that . . . ." Doha turned toward me with a questioning look, but I was unable to complete my sentence. Still, she registered my finger pointing at the upholstered door and my infuriated stance. Suddenly she broke into a smile and studied me the way she used to so long ago.

19

Turning into one of the Ministry corridors, I spotted Sayyid al-Qinawi speaking to a group of gray-uniformed janitorial staff. He was visibly upset. As I approached, the workers moved aside to clear a path for me and stood staring silently at the floor.

Gesturing at the circle of men around him, Sayyid said, "Do you know what happened, sir? Someone persuaded them to tell the investigators that they went to Port Said. None of them have ever set foot there, but they're going to say that they've been to Port Said and were put up in a five star hotel." He laughed abjectly.

I turned to the workers. "Why? From what I understood, Sayyid stuck his neck out for you. That embezzled money was meant for you. It was your right. So why are you deserting him?"

A withered gray-haired man pointed an accusing finger at Sayyid and, ignoring me and addressing him, said, "Now listen here. You get to fly off to Europe and America. And you've done the pilgrimage to Mecca. Everybody's got to look out for himself."

I had never seen Sayyid so angry. The muscles in his face tensed, the veins in his neck bulged, and his hands were bunched into fists. I was sure he was going to punch the old man. But he gained control over himself and said in a low, taut voice, "Now you listen, old man. I made the pilgrimage on this here." He rapped several times on his wooden leg, the knocking muffled by the fabric of his trousers. Still fighting to keep his voice in check, he added, "Did someone tell you I'm a thief? That I come back from abroad with gifts for my superiors so they'll send me on another trip? That I take stipends from committees? Are rumors going around that I . . . ." Then he burst out, "If you don't stand up for yourselves, who will?"

Another worker replied. Shaking his head dejectedly, he said, "God will stand by us, Sayyid. We're just not up to the Deputy Minister. He holds our jobs in his hands."

I took hold of Sayyid's elbow and led him away from the group. "Don't blame them, Sayyid," I said softly. "As they said, they're worried about their jobs."

"No, that's not what it's about. It's about greed. It's about 'Kill me tomorrow, but let me live today,' as the saying goes. Your brother-in-law Abd al-Magid handed them five pounds each to testify that they went to Port Said, and he gave them backdated receipts to show to the investigators as proof."

He paused abruptly and looked at me for a moment. Then he said, "You were right, sir. I plunged in way out of my depth. Everybody knows that the country belongs to the likes of Sultan Bek and Madam Doha. Even the people in the Socialist Union asked me to withdraw my complaint and settle the matter with Sultan Bek." He slapped his palms together despairingly. "They tell us to fight corruption wherever we see it. Then when you show them the proof they say, 'We can't afford chaos on the domestic front. Submit a report and let the government take care of it.' " He gripped my arm. "I'm not the type who submits reports. I'm not a spy, like you suggested once. I speak my mind. But what's the point? The government says it wants one thing when it wants another, and the people say they want one thing when they want another. What's Abdel Nasser supposed to do? And me, who's nobody, what am I supposed to do? I give up!"

"Please, don't give up, Sayyid. You've only just begun," I said to soothe him. We were near Hatem's office, so I suggested we go in and speak with him.

Sayyid let go of my arm and laughed bitterly. "Mr. Hatem gave up a long time ago. He doesn't want to get involved. He talks and talks, but when things get serious he looks after himself. Mr. Hatem's sane, like you and everyone else." He turned and limped off down the corridor, moving rapidly but laboriously, propping his hand to the wall every few steps to keep his balance.

I went in to see Hatem anyway. He was thinner than the last time I had seen him. He welcomed me pleasantly, but there was a slight tremor in his hands and he sounded nervous. I started to relate to him what had happened with Sayyid, but he cut me off.

"I know, I know. I know how much each of the workers took and where that money came from. Even the money that Sultan Bek and his gang are using to save their hides was embezzled from the ministry budget."

"So, as long as you know all that, what do you think should be done about it?"

"Nothing," he answered firmly. "This isn't like that business about getting paid on Fridays. Back then Sayyid was dealing with the government at large, which is to say with no one in particular. This time he landed himself in the serpents' pit. They're all powerful men and they are all in it together—in the ministry, in the Socialist Union, everywhere. When I told that to Sayyid, he said, 'When you cut off the head of a serpent it dies. Get Sultan Bek and the ministry will be clean again.' But that's not true."

His hands were knotted together and jerking up and down continuously in rhythm with his speech. He avoided looking me in the face.

"But what about you? Why don't you try to do something? Sayyid said you've changed. Is it because of Doha?"

He shook his head emphatically. "No. I don't see her anymore, if that's what bothers you. And I haven't forgotten her either, as though it's any business of yours. But she's not the reason."

"Then why are you telling me this now, Hatem? This wasn't the way you spoke when you joined the Liberation Rally. You stuck with it. Believe me, even though I quit politics a part of me was proud that one of us was still trying. So why are you throwing in the towel now, and leaving Sayyid and me in the lurch—and yourself, too?"

"Why now? Because I've realized that the serpent will never die. We're fighting in vain because it's coiled around the earth." He returned to his place behind his desk and began rapping the desktop with his fingertips as he spoke. "This problem's been bothering me for a long time, since the days I was working on my postgraduate studies. That's why I dropped law and took up history. I kept asking myself why it had to be this way. I was determined to try everything and never give up. But I discovered that injustice is invincible. So what's the solution? Revolution? Angry people led by revolutionaries who promise them justice and the golden age? Who begin by cutting off the serpent's head, as Sayyid puts it? The fact is, it doesn't matter whether that head's called Louis XVI of France or Farouk I of Egypt, or Nuri al-Said of Iraq. Contrary to the common impression, the body doesn't die. It stays alive. It lurks underground, subtly mutating. It sprouts twenty heads to replace the one that was cut off, and it rises again. One of those heads is, 'Safeguard the revolution from its enemies.' Whether it goes by the name Robespierre or Beria it aims its lethal sting precisely at the friends of the revolution. Another head is 'Stability,' in the name of which everything reverts to exactly the way it was before the revolution. Eventually, the serpent rears a brand new head. Whether it calls itself Caliph Yazid Bin Mu'awiya, Napoleon Bonaparte, or Stalin, this is the head that crowns the new order of tyranny, parading beneath the emblem, 'the welfare of the people.' 'The welfare of the people,' in turn, is quickly reduced to 'temporary exigencies,' the byword for that 'interim' phase of repression necessary for the revolution to accomplish its mission. Under such conditions, advocates of justice acquire another name—'leftists,' 'reactionaries,' 'heretics,' 'enemies of the people'—depending upon the circumstances."

138

He regarded me with bloodshot eyes. "I used to think that all it would take for my family to see a brighter future was for the country to be put right. But, as I've discovered, that's not enough; the whole world has to be put right, and that's impossible. Tell Sayyid that he'd better learn a very important lesson: the serpent never dies."

"I won't tell him anything of the sort," I said as I stood to leave. "He's depressed enough as it is. But do you know what, Hatem? Maybe he's the only one of us who's got it right. Sure, he probably can't save the advocates of justice and he probably won't kill the serpent, but at least he's saving his soul."

"Even if he destroys himself in the process?"

I paused for a moment at the door. "Yes," I answered. "Tell me, what caused that scar on your forehead? The bullet could have penetrated your skull. You could have died in the course of your demand for justice. Yes, I know that the quest for justice is a disease, but it's the only disease that doesn't afflict animals. It all boils down to the fact that you and I have been cured, which is why we can see the symptoms in others."

Hatem did not respond. He had tilted his head toward the window and was staring absently at the roof of the broadcasting building, which was filled with soldiers, sheltered behind walls of sandbags, helmets snug on their heads.

I did not return to the coffeehouse that day. Nor to my office. I felt tired, so I went home. When I opened the door I caught sight of Abd al-Magid scurrying out of my bedroom. When I went in there, I found all my drawers open and my papers scattered over the floor. I stormed out. Abd al-Magid stood outside my bedroom door, arms folded across his chest. Samira stood next to him. Before I could open my mouth, he shouted, "Your sister's going to have a baby and we have to protect ourselves! What if they raided the apartment and searched your room? God knows what you have in those papers of yours!"

I walked steadily toward him as he spoke. Then I swung at him, putting not just the full length of my arm, but the weight of my whole body into the blow. He yelped and reeled back. I moved in again and began to punch him, Samira all the while screaming at me to stop. He fought back, striking out at my face and stomach. I wrestled him to the ground and pinned him to the floor. I bellowed, "Is that why you were searching my room, Abd al-Magid? Or were you looking for something Sultan Bek could use?" I grabbed hold of his shirt and pulled him to his feet. Curses and threats spat from his ashen face. I dragged him to the front door, flung it open and shouted, "Don't ever set foot in this house again!"

Samira rushed to brace herself in front of the open door. "This is my house as much as it's yours! It's my father's house!" she yelled. I moved toward her. Her eyes widened at some expression she saw at my face, and she slid out of the way and began screaming again.

I shoved Abd al-Magid out the door and turned to her. "I've put up with you and your father for too long. Forty years. That's more than enough. And the serpent's lived here way too long, too. The door's wide open, Samira. Go with him, if you want."

I heard her shoes clicking down the stairs as she called out anxiously, "Abd al-Magid! Abd al-Magid!"

I closed the door and went back to my bedroom to examine the mess he had made with my papers. I tried to recall whether they had contained anything to do with Sayyid al-Qinawi.

20

It was too late for Sayyid to withdraw from the case even if he had wanted to. The wheels of the investigation were turning, and he was constantly being called in for questioning. After all, he was the one who had filed the complaint and submitted the documents. We met nearly every day, either in my office or in the ministry building, in order to work out what he should tell the panels or to consult with friends in the legal departments. To our surprise, many stepped forward with advice or to volunteer additional information that could be used against the Deputy Minister. Still, everything was working in Sultan Bek's favor. The workers testified under oath that they had left Cairo for Port Said on the Thursday afternoon at issue and returned on the evening of the following Friday, and they submitted the forged receipts as evidence. The owner of the hotel in Port Said testified that the workers had spent the night in his hotel and showed the investigators the hotel register with the names of the workers listed next to rooms they occupied for the night in question. The Ministry's accounts director testified that all the workers had paid the nominal twenty-five-piaster registration fee, and he produced the paperwork indicating the dates these payments were received and entered into accounts.

The results of the case seemed a foregone conclusion. Moreover, Sultan Bek's minions were now flitting around the offices, putting it about that Sayyid was going to be prosecuted on the charge of filing malicious allegations, and that he and the retrograde elements that had spurred him on would probably be locked away in order to purge the ministry and the rest of the country of their evil.

But there was one small glimmer of light. A separate inquiry was being held with the tourist company that purportedly arranged the trip to Port Said, and the deputy public prosecutor in charge of this investigation was resolved to handle it in his own way: he was interested in the truth. Having learned that the company's bus not only did not take the workers to Port Said or anywhere else but had never left the garage that Thursday, he concluded that all the documentation submitted by the ministry accounts department pertaining to transportation expenses was forged. His finding rekindled the ministry's internal investigation, and new deputy prosecutors were put in charge of the case.

Sayyid came to the office to tell me this news. He was barely able to control the emotional tremor in his voice as he said, "Do you know what I prayed for when I held the curtains on the Kaaba? I asked God over and over again to help me beat the oppressors. And look what happened. Who would have ever believed that the truth would come out?"

Fearful that he was in for another shock, I cautioned him to wait until the investigators issued their report. "It's too early to celebrate, Sayyid. It isn't over yet," I said.

He imparted another piece of news that day. As he was leaving, he paused at the door and said, "Something must have happened to your friend, Madam Doha, because of all this."

My heart thumped. I cried out anxiously in spite of myself, "What happened? What happened to Doha?"

He chuckled. "I think this whole business has affected her mind. Usually, when she comes across me in the Ministry, she passes without saying a word. She's too high and mighty to talk to the likes of me. But today, when she saw me, she actually stopped and spoke to me. She said, 'Sayyid, you're an Atris,' or an Idris, or something like that. I said, 'God forgive you,' and left her standing there. I don't get into fights with women. What are women to us anyway? We're fighting the serpent and we're going to cut off its head."

He pealed with laughter as he hobbled off down the corridor. It had been a long time since I had heard him laugh. But it was not just that that made me smile. Contrary to what he had imagined, Doha had not hurled an insult at him. True to her erudition, she had alluded to a legendary Arab hero.

As I was closing the shutters preparatory to leaving the office that afternoon, I heard approaching footsteps echo off the walls of the vacant antechamber. I knew immediately that it was her. The footsteps brought to mind her familiar fragrance and the sound of raindrops. I turned and saw her standing at the threshold of the half-darkened office in which she hadn't set foot since that distant day when she had packed up her papers and left. I stood rooted in my place next to the window, staring at the tall, slender figure in the doorway with the halo of black hair around her face. Since only the faintest shafts of light penetrated through the shutters her features remained obscure. Instinctively I reached out to reopen one of the shutters to let in more light. She was wearing a white dress and a black handbag hung from a long strap over her shoulder.

"May I come in?" she asked from the doorway.

In a barely audible voice I answered, "I let you in once before, Doha, and you destroyed my life. But come in."

She took a few steps into the room, glanced at the empty space where her desk once stood, and said, "You're all alone here now."

"Yes, completely alone."

She took a seat on one of the two chairs in front of my desk, and I sat down facing her and the half-open window behind her. A faint smile played on her lips as she studied me. Her face was pale, but it was free of all makeup. I looked at her plucked eyebrows and mentally filled them to their former thickness, bringing back the Doha of years ago.

Still smiling enigmatically, she said, "You hate me now, of course."

"You've done all that you could to make me hate you, but I still can't."

Her eyes shifted to the spot where her desk had stood. "I came to say goodbye. I handed in my resignation today. Or, to be precise, Sultan Bek asked me to resign. I'm supposed to take the fall for him."

"That's not surprising, not after everything that's happened."

"Yes, it's not surprising," she repeated softly.

The sound of the window creaking open drew my attention. I focused on the view outside so as to avoid looking at her. A kite, hovering in the blue sky over the building opposite, flapped its wings and soared into the distance then sailed into view again, its wings outstretched and still.

Suddenly, as I sat there, adrift, inert, numbed by that inextinguishable love, a wave of pent up rage surged within me. "Why Doha?" I shouted. "Why the theft, the gambling den, all that corruption?" My anger was violent, irrepressible. "Why did you leave me so suddenly? Why did you refuse to marry me? I wasn't the evil Faust you said I was, and you weren't the innocent girl being led to her death. We were being sucked down the vortex together, but we could have rescued ourselves together. Why did you run away? Why did you torture Hatem? Why did you try to ruin Sayyid? Are you part of the body of the serpent that never dies? Is there any part of Aset left? Have you left even a bit of her beautiful dream intact?"

The questions fired out of my mouth without expecting answers from that woman in white. In the semi-darkness of the room, the purse at her side seemed to form a solitary black wing. I realized my questions were aimed at persons unknown, but there was no stopping them. When they finally petered out, Doha looked down and said, "Aset has gone. She left when we were in Rome and maybe even before that. She's gone." She lifted her pallid face to me. "And when she left, she took all the flowers and trees with her." She raised her hand in front of her face. "She took away my sight. Now trees and flowers mean nothing more to me than wooden posts and shriveled petals."

"But why, Doha?"

She looked around as though she might find the answer there in that room. Then softly as though speaking to herself, she said. "I know she's still alive. Her evil brother Set has brought her to the ground, but in her exile she is still searching for Osiris. Pieces of her fall off whenever she loses her way—she, too, is becoming scattered limbs. But when she finds Osiris she will be made whole again. She will take wing again and her bowels will give birth to a young and vigorous hawk, a perfect hawk. And it will fly before her, its fiery eyes chasing Set from every corner of the earth. And she will fly behind it, a proud, white steed soaring over the yellow desert, and everywhere she alights crops will sprout and trees will flourish."

Her black eyes shone as they fixed on mine. "Aset has left. But she will return." Her eyes moistened, but no tears fell.

I was still confused. "But why did Aset leave, Doha, and when will she return?"

She spread her hands open, palms up, and tried to smile as she said softly, "One doesn't ask Aset when, and one doesn't ask her why."

At that moment, both shutters flew open, filling the room with daylight. Every feature of hers was completely distinct. Her honey-colored face was still wan, but it glowed with an ageless beauty.